V is for...
VAMPIRE

A
VAMPIRE ISLAND
STORY

Also by
ADELE GRIFFIN

Vampire Island

The Knaveheart's Curse

V IS FOR... VAMPIRE

A
VAMPIRE ISLAND
STORY

ADELE GRIFFIN

G. P. PUTNAM'S SONS
PENGUIN YOUNG READERS GROUP

G. P. PUTNAM'S SONS
A division of Penguin Young Readers Group.
Published by The Penguin Group.
Penguin Group (USA) Inc., 375 Hudson Street, New York, NY 10014, U.S.A.
Penguin Group (Canada), 90 Eglinton Avenue East, Suite 700, Toronto,
Ontario M4P 2Y3, Canada (a division of Pearson Penguin Canada Inc.).
Penguin Books Ltd, 80 Strand, London WC2R 0RL, England.
Penguin Ireland, 25 St. Stephen's Green, Dublin 2, Ireland
(a division of Penguin Books Ltd.).
Penguin Group (Australia), 250 Camberwell Road, Camberwell, Victoria 3124, Australia
(a division of Pearson Australia Group Pty Ltd).
Penguin Books India Pvt Ltd, 11 Community Centre, Panchsheel Park,
New Delhi—110 017, India.
Penguin Group (NZ), 67 Apollo Drive, Rosedale, North Shore 0632, New Zealand
(a division of Pearson New Zealand Ltd).
Penguin Books (South Africa) (Pty) Ltd, 24 Sturdee Avenue,
Rosebank, Johannesburg 2196, South Africa.
Penguin Books Ltd, Registered Offices: 80 Strand, London WC2R 0RL, England.

Library of Congress Cataloging-in-Publication Data
Griffin, Adele. V is for—vampire : a Vampire Island story / Adele Griffin.   p. cm.
Summary: Lexie Livingstone, a vampire-human hybrid living in New York City and trying
to gain mortality, faces typical ninth-grade dramas like boys and school politics, as well
as not-so-typical obstacles like obnoxious pixie houseguests. [1. Vampires—Fiction. 2.
Pixies—Fiction. 3. Elections—Fiction. 4. Politics, Practical—Fiction. 5. Friendship—Fiction.
6. High schools—Fiction. 7. Schools—Fiction. 8. New York (N.Y.)—Fiction.] I. Title.
PZ7.G881325Vaak 2009   [Fic]—dc22   2009007487
ISBN 978-0-399-25277-8
1 3 5 7 9 10 8 6 4 2

For Sara

1

SO GOOD, IT'S SICK

I've got gossip!" announced Lexie Livingstone. She and her best friend, Pete Stubbe, were enjoying lunch—a peanut-butter-and-pickle sandwich for Pete and a four-berry medley for Lexie—in the school's courtyard. Parrish High School kids were allowed to eat lunch outside until it got too cold. But today, New York City weather was mellow, with just a nip of autumn in the air.

Pete stopped chewing. "Tell me!" His yellow eyes gleamed.

"Mina Pringle called me last night and—" Lexie swallowed back an excitement hiccup. "She wants me to write speeches for her campaign to be ninth-grade class president."

"Congratulations. You've lost your mind," said Pete. "Why would you want to write speeches for your enemy?"

"Pete!" Lexie reached out to pinch Pete's arm.

"Don't you get it? Mina Pringle has finished being suspicious of my hybrid-vampire ways. She wants to be my friend. She's waving the olive branch. She's burying the hatchet. She's—"

"She's sneakier than a diamond-backed python," said Pete, "and I haven't trusted her since fourth-grade show-

and-tell, when she told the class she was the heiress to a potato-chip fortune. It's the only time I can remember when a kid had to apologize for making a false show-and-tell statement."

He shook his head in disgust as he peeled the crust from his bread in a single curl. Then—making sure nobody was looking—he used his advanced werewolf powers to fling the crust far over the iron gate, all the way across Central Park to FDR Drive, where a skinny stray dog was snuffling for lunch. The dog yipped for joy as he snapped up the snack.

Lexie crunched her lunch bag and popped in her retainer. "Don't be that way, Pete. Remember, 'Jealousy is the jaundice of the soul.' " While Lexie could always trust herself to find the perfect quote, she also knew that jealousy was part of Pete's werewolf identity since wolves are territorial and don't like to share anything.

Especially not friends.

"Working on a campaign is kind of a big deal," continued Lexie, "especially since Mr. Fellows wants us to learn about politics. There'll be some major debates and stump speeches and—"

"Yeah, yeah, I know all about it. I'm voting for Neil Needleburger. That phony Mina Pringle would make a human stinkbug of a president. And if you weren't so blinded by wanting her to like you, you'd see that, too."

From the look in Pete's eye, Lexie decided it would be best to drop the whole subject. And Pete wasn't the only kid in the school who didn't adore Mina.

Later, walking home from school, Lexie decided that, going forward, she'd keep her Mina friendship separate from her Pete friendship. After all, Pete had every right to be jealous. Lexie and Pete had been BFFs since the Livingstones had arrived in the New World five years ago, ready to trade their old identities as bloodsuckers for the higher hope of turning human. The Stubbes had just moved from the Old World, too, and were trying to rid themselves of their wolfish ways. Lexie was the only hybrid vampire and Pete was the only hybrid werewolf in their whole school, and their unusual powers were their biggest secret from the rest of the class. So they had a lot in common.

R U free? Lexie's cell phone buzzed the text message. Her heart raced. She knew that number.

YES!! she wrote back.

1057 CPW / 15D

K! Lexie texted, turning a sharp V as she switched direction, heading for Central Park West. Quickly, she wrote her parents to tell them that she was dropping by Mina's apartment for a school project.

Crossing Central Park, her large, black-booted feet kicking up piles of wet yellow leaves, Lexie turned up her face to the sun. This was the first fall that she'd been able to bask in sunshine. No more cringing from the light of day. No more reaching for the XPF, prescription-strength sunblock. Yes, those old vampire traits were dying off. She'd worked hard, and she'd earned it.

My mortality, Lexie mused poetically, is like a fresh coat of paint over my cracked and peeling vampire soul.

3

Unlike her little sister, Maddy, or her kid brother, Hudson, careful Lexie always had focused intently on her human studies. She hardly ever used any of the vamp tricks that the Argos frowned upon. By next summer, she might just be ready to wear that sequin-trim bikini she'd bought two years ago as inspiration. Which would be right on time for Mina Pringle's annual Fourth of July roof-deck party, which Lexie had never been invited to.

In fact, for the past five years, Lexie had overheard the supercool girls talk way too much about Mina's swanky get-togethers, posh birthday bashes, and exclusive slumber parties. Now here I am, thought Lexie as leaves fluttered up in front of her like startled butterflies. In with the in crowd! I'm Mina Pringle's speechwriter!

Seriously, this was a big deal.

Of course, Mina is lucky to have me, too, Lexie reminded herself as she rode the fancy elevator in Mina's building to the fifteenth floor. My health essay on dark leafy greens was nothing short of magnificent. My biology report on the dating habits of snails versus slugs could only be termed thrilling. And who will forget my extra-credit, after-school presentation on the short life of doomed urban vampire poet Fun K. Blood?

Though the only person who would never forget it was Pete, since he was the only one who'd shown up to hear it.

The little kid who opened 15D's door looked like Mina but younger. Same ballerina legs, same yellow curls, same pout. "Meeen-a!" she yelled. "There's a super-skinny, scary-pale girlie out here. Is she your friend?"

4

"That's my speechwriter," called Mina, amid a babble of other chatting voices, most of whom Lexie recognized from school. "Let her in, Nina."

Nina allowed the door to swing open, and Lexie followed Nina's lemony-curly head through the apartment. Such a contrast to the Livingstones' spooky townhouse, which her family had inherited after her sister, Maddy, had sent the previous, evil vampire owners crumbling to their deaths.

The Livingstone house was dark and mildewy and smelled like feet. The Pringle home was airy and fragrant and smelled like peaches.

My vampire heritage can be a real drag, grumped Lexie. There's nothing chic about my creepy house, my fangs, my ew-normous, double-jointed hands and feet, and having people like Nina Pringle look at me like I'm a three-headed spider.

At least the rest of her classmates didn't act so horrified to see her.

"Hi, Lexie," they chorused once Lexie was deposited in a chair in the middle of the Pringles' plushy, peachy velvet den, where all Mina's friends, including her best friend, Lucy "Loo" Susskind, were creating poster boards for Mina's campaign.

"Hey, not so fast." Mina spun Lexie's wheeled chair around and pushed her toward a desk in the darkest corner of the den, far from the others. "You're my speechwriter. You need peace and quiet. I want you to have the best, peacefulest spot in the room."

"Thanks." And then, because she couldn't resist, Lexie

quoted, "'The art of being kind / Is all the sad world needs.'" Though she couldn't help a longing look at the other girls or reaching out to snatch a crumb-top peach bar from a tray as she wheeled past. The world was certainly less sad if you were eating a peach bar.

The old Mina would have squawked in disgust at Lexie's split-second, peach-reaching reflexes. This Mina just smiled. "My speech really needs some tweaks," she confessed. "It's not flowery enough. That's where you come in. You're so good at frilly writing, it's sick."

Lexie blushed at the compliment. To be sick at something was Mina's highest praise.

"I'll try," she said modestly. She peered at the computer monitor. On the screen were the words:

What I Can Do for Parrish High School!
By Mina Pringle
If Elected to Ninth-Grade Class President,
I, Wilhelmina Arabella Pringle, Do Solemnly
Swear

The rest of the page was blank.

"How cute is my choice of font?" asked Mina. "It's called Lucida Calligraphy. Isn't it sooo sweet?"

"Sooo sweet!" hollered Loo from the other side of the room.

"Where's the rest of your speech?" asked Lexie.

Mina tapped her temple. "Up here. I was thinking that

I could just hit you with some of my *fantastical* ideas, and then, presto, you make them into sentences."

"Sure. Ready when you are." Lexie's long fingers hovered on the keyboard. She wondered if Neil Needleburger had his own speechwriter. The vote would be the populars against the nerds. Lexie would never admit it, but she felt torn. She was in honor society, took karate class, and was on the debate team with Neil. He was a nice, nerdy guy. More importantly, he loved government and would make a smart and careful class president.

"Ahem. My ideas." Mina cleared her throat. "The big four." She counted on her fingers. "One, I want the vending machine to sell Fizzle Nuts. Two, I want a splashing fountain in front of the school. Three, I want baby ducks in that fountain. Four, I want Principal Oliphant to fire our crabby crossing guard, Mrs. Yoder."

"Mrs. Yoder can't be fired," said Lexie. "She's a volunteer."

"She's cranky."

"She was the bus driver for forty years. Now she's too old to drive, but she likes to stay part of the school."

"Well, maybe the school doesn't want *her* part of *it*." But then Mina waved away the argument. "Whatever, work with my top three. Until I think up another one. Put it into some paragraphs, and I'll check your copy, honey."

Lexie loved writing, and she really loved how Mina called her "honey." Eventually Lexie forgot about everything else—such as the fact that she was sitting all by herself. How could she crack this speech? Mina's ideas were odd . . . but maybe if she focused on *why* Parrish High School should have a fountain with baby ducks . . .

"What *is* this, anyway?"

Lexie looked up, blinking. Mina was sitting there reading Lexie's private PHOLD book. (PHOLD stood for *p*oems, *h*opes, *o*pinions, *l*yrics, and *d*reams—and Lexie had a lot of all of these. In fact, this was her thirteenth PHOLD edition.) Lexie couldn't believe it—Mina must have gone through her backpack.

"Just my notebook," Lexie said. Her fingers itched to snatch back the book. But in the spirit of her new friendship with Mina, she didn't want to seem uptight.

"It's filled with slurpy goop," said Mina, as if Lexie didn't know.

Lexie tried to look casual as she reached for the book. "Okay, I'll take it now—oh, no, please, please don't keep reading it."

But Mina gripped tight. "Concentrate on your speech, dear. Don't mind me." Smilingly, with one hand, she offered Lexie a second peach bar while the other hand kept hold of the PHOLD.

"Um, okay." Lexie dropped the argument, and the PHOLD, to bite into baked fruit sweetness. She *had* wanted another peach bar—it was like Mina could read her thoughts. It was sick what good friends they were already.

Besides, there was nothing especially secret in her PHOLD book, Lexie concluded as she watched Mina sink back into a chair, reading intently. Mostly eighth-grade-y stuff, plus a few song lyrics from this past summer, when Lexie had taken up the guitar. Maybe it was time to share her notebook.

And if Mina was impressed by the PHOLD, that would be a bonus. She'd give anything to make Mina forget about that shameful moment, back in fourth grade, when she'd picked her nose with her tongue. Such a silly, kiddie vamp trick. Thankfully, tongue-to-nose picking was years behind her, and the future looked as bright as some of her notebook's dreams.

Especially if the future meant hanging out with the marvelously popular, most perfect of the perf crowd Mina Pringle. In fact, a friendship with Mina seemed like just about the least vampire-ish thing that Lexie could gain. It was hard not to want it as much as humanly possible.

2

AN ELECTRIC ANNOUNCEMENT

Okay, Maddy. I give up. What the holy hopscotch are you doing in that outfit?" Lexie's mother had spoken first, but really everyone wanted to know.

Four sets of brown eyes—Lexie's, her mother's, her father's, and her younger brother Hudson's—were all trained on Lexie's little sister.

Maddy was dressed in a white nurse's uniform that had been spattered from head to toe with blobs of crusting ketchup.

"I'm Nurse Hatchet," announced Maddy. "And here's my winning costume catchphrase. Ready?" She picked up her rubber-tipped hatchet, which was from Hudson's Viking costume from last Halloween. "When Nurse Hatchet works the night shift, it's a bloody emergency!" Then she reached forward and chop-chop-chopped the leftover vegetable quiche from dinner. Spinach went flying. A blob smacked Lexie between the eyes. "Dudes, isn't this an excellent Halloween costume?"

"More than half of us are not 'dudes,'" corrected Maddy's mother.

"Also, mind your manners." Lexie wiped her face. How could she ever invite Mina Pringle over to her house when

Maddy would ruin it? A bratty little sister was one thing. A bratty little half-vampire sister who wielded a rubber hatchet was a whole different bag of blood.

"Maddy, it's only the first week of October," said Hudson. "You're almost thirty days ahead of Halloween."

"Yeah, but Halloween is such a freaking incredible holiday that I decided to make October an entire Hallo-month," Maddy declared. "And every day of Hallo-month, I'm gonna be wearing a different costume. Now aren't you grateful to be related to the brilliant Madison Livingstone? You're welcome." Her eyes twinkled.

"Your teachers will let you be in costume all month?" asked Lexie's father.

"Not exactly," said Maddy. "But I've got it worked out. I'll wear my costume on the bus to school, then change out of it for class, then change back into it for recess till I get caught—which I won't—then change into my uniform for sports, then change back in after—"

Pop! The house went black.

Eeeeeeeeeek! Lights-out! We're in trouble! Lexie shrieked, not using her voice, but her bat skills of echolocation, to bounce the message to Hudson. Lights-out meant a visit from the Argos. And the Argos—who were the Livingstones' liaisons between the Old World, from which they'd fled, and the New World, where they now lived as almost "normal humans"—came calling only when the news was bad.

They've got nothing on me. I've been following all the vamp rules, bounced Hudson.

Me too, bounced Maddy. *I haven't slain a mosquito in like six days. And Orville's used to me messing up on the bug-blood issue.*

Maybe it's just a power outage, Lexie bounced.

But when the sconces flickered on again, Orville of the Argos was perched on the dining room table candelabra.

Orville was an ancient, owl-like creature. By day, he worked in human form at Maddy and Hudson's school as a janitor, where he kept watch on his world without being much noticed himself. As Orville of the Argos, he was their spokes-creature, and his words were their law. So when he spoke, the Livingstones listened, even if his voice was as scratchy as a dry leaf blowing down a drainpipe.

"What have we done, Orville?" Even Lexie's mother looked puzzled.

Orville held up a crackled claw. "Nothing," he rasped. "In fact, you Livingstones have been exemplary. Obedient to all the New World rules," he said, with a doubtful glance at Maddy. "And I'm confident that some of you will soon achieve your dreams of fullblood mortality and leave this vestige vampire nonsense behind."

Under the table, Lexie crossed her extra-long fingers. She hoped Orville was talking about her especially. After all, Maddy and even Hudson had way too much vamp in them, what with Maddy's bloodsucking ways and Hudson's love of flying.

"If we've been so good," spoke Lexie's father, "then why are you here, Orville?"

"Yes, yes. I'm coming to that." Orville frilled his neck ruff and reached up to peck some spinach off the chandelier. "I need to offer two Old Worlders a place to stay while their New World home and jobs are prepared upstate. Like you, they've become weary of the Old World and want a change of pace."

Everyone breathed a sigh of relief. Vampire Relocation Services was simple. The Livingstones had helped out in the VRS department plenty of times.

"We welcome our ancient vampire kin," said Lexie's father. "Matter of fact, I just bought two new inflatable coffins. They're somewhere down in the basement. I'll just need to find the air pump, then we'll be—"

"No, no, no. These guests aren't vamps. And it's only for a week or so." Orville chewed his claw.

Bad sign, thought Lexie. What did he want to come out and say? Vampires, no. But from the Old World, yes . . . Lexie mulled over different possibilities.

Werewolves? No, all Werewolf Relocation Services went to Pete Stubbe's family. Ghouls? No. Most ghouls headed straight from the Old World to hang in the swampy Florida Everglades. Goblins and druids? No, druids and goblins liked the country. Selkies? No. Selkies liked the sea.

"I don't get it," said Lexie. "Who are they?"

Orville had gone from flustered to downright jittery. "As a matter of fact, they are, um, pixies," he said. "Sorry. You're the only ones I thought could handle them. It's only for a week or so. Well, guess that's it. Gotta dash."

Pop! The lights went out again. When they snapped back on, Orville had disappeared. Nobody at the table could speak from shock.

Pixies, eek! In the Old World, they were considered the wildest houseguests of all—and with good reason, Lexie remembered. A couple of hundred years ago, Lexie's uncle Mortimer and his pix wife, Bijou, had visited the Livingstones. Bijou had taught them the limbo and how to make crepes flambé, but she'd also hidden the teaspoons, mixed the salt with sugar, and stolen the buttons off their clothes.

It had been an exhausting weekend.

Of course, the rules were different here. Here, all ex–Old Worlders had to be on their best behavior if they wanted to stay. That was the deal, and Lexie was pretty sure that pixies were no exception.

So why were Orville's feathers in such a ruffle?

3

O PINING POETESS

*F*inally," Mina read, "for many centuries, the fountain has been a symbol of luck, friendship, and knowledge. Is there any better way to welcome friends and visitors to Parrish High School than with this symbol, splashing brightly right outside our school's front door?"

In her front-row desk, Lexie mouthed along with Mina as she recited Lexie's speech for the rest of the ninth-grade classroom.

"If we pitch in with fund-raising," continued Mina (and Lexie), "we can make this dream come true. Also, all future coins tossed into this fountain will go to establish Parrish's very own . . . poetry department?"

Mina's voice trailed off into a question at the last sentence. She frowned and flipped the page. Lexie held her breath, watching Mina's eyes scan the speech for all that nasty stuff that Mina had insisted Lexie put in about poor Mrs. Yoder. At the last minute, Lexie had deleted it and added her own brilliant idea for the poetry department.

But if Mina was mad, she didn't look it. She looked confident. She pushed aside her speech and rested her elbows on the podium. "One last thing. If I am your class president, I, Wilhelmina Pringle, do solemnly swear to get rid of icky Mrs. Yoder. My sources tell me she doesn't even work here. That's right, Yoder's only a volunteer! So if Yoder can bully her way into this school for free, well, let's toss her right back out again, no charge. Access denied!" She slammed the flat of her hand like a gavel against the wood.

In the back of the room, Mina's friends cheered and applauded.

"You may sit down now, Mina," said Mr. Fellows. "Next speech, no mudslinging. Crossing guards and volunteers deserve our respect, and Mrs. Yoder is both."

"Uh-oh, we're twice cursed." Mina made a face, and everyone laughed.

Lexie saw Neil Needleburger mop his damp forehead. Unfortunately, Neil's speech had been sweet, smart, and sooo dreary. Even Lexie had sneaked out some of her chemistry homework to finish right in the middle of it.

"Ace speechwriting, honey," said Mina as she caught up with Lexie in the hall later that day. "That coins-in-the-fountain touch was cute—but I think we should use those coins to fund an adorable little spa instead, for post–gym workouts." She snapped her fingers. "Oops! I forgot to say my idea number five, to change our school mascot from Boris the Brown Badger to Kaylee Milquetoast." She shook back her curls. "But I think I clinched it."

"Oh, yes, you totally clinched it," crooned Loo. "Kaylee Milquetoast would be the fantastickest school mascot. She's my favorite pop singer–actress–model in the whole, entire—"

"Mina?"

Lexie's heart bounced. Dylan Easterby was standing behind them. Over the summer, Dylan had shot up so tall that he and Lexie were now the same height. Which meant that they both looked down at Mina.

"Yes?" Dylan's tallness made Mina look extra cute. But same-size couples were also cute, weren't they? Lexie had to hold on to that hope.

Lexie could hardly remember a time when she wasn't in love with hunky Dylan. She'd even sent him a postcard this summer called "Ode to My Amber-Eyed Athlete" that was so chock-full of pent-up Dylan-y desire, she hadn't been brave enough to sign her name to the bottom.

They'd been back at school for over a month, and Dylan still hadn't asked her about it, so she guessed maybe he hadn't recognized her handwriting or her ruby red, lip-sticked kiss print.

Maybe if I recite a single line, thought Lexie, then Dylan will recognize me as the pining poetess?

"O Easter would be joyous, if Easterby were mine—" she began softly, but Dylan was already talking to Mina.

"Thanks for that note you put in my locker," he said. "It was . . . inspiring."

Note? What inspiring note? Lexie's blood raised a couple of degrees. Mina could pick a cute font easy, but she could barely stack two words together. Something was up.

"Sure, Dylan. Anytime." Mina's voice was music. Her special Dylan-loving voice. The old Lexie—the one who

17

had been enemies with Mina—had always hated that voice. "Catch up with you later?"

"No prob. Bye, Mina. Bye, Loo, bye, Lex." Dylan paused, as if he might want to say something extra to Lexie. She waited, breath held. But then all he did was amble off to rejoin his friends.

"Poor Dylan. He was freaking out about soccer," explained Mina. "So I had to psych him up. You know how it is."

"Totally," agreed Loo.

"I'll stop by your house after my ballet lesson this afternoon to get your ideas for the next speech." Mina rewarded Lexie with a dimpled smile. "Okay, honey?"

"No problem," Lexie managed.

But on the way home from school, she couldn't hold in her jealousy. "Pete, answer honestly. Is Mina Pringle *inspiring*?"

"Mina Pringle is an air-breathing land slug," answered Pete, "and, sadly, she's going to slither her way to victory over Neil Needleburger in this election. Poor Needler. The kid's such a policy wonk, and he hasn't got a chance."

"Dylan Easterby's a rock star on the soccer field. He doesn't need Mina's inspiration." Lexie fumed. She couldn't rid her mind of that scene at school. Dylan had seemed so . . . *impressed* by Mina. What could she possibly have written? And why hadn't Lexie thought of it instead? There had to be a thousand poetic sentiments for "psyching up" an athlete that she could have written for Dylan. A spunky sonnet for practice. A plucky couplet for victory. An airy haiku for defeat.

Lexie's fingertips itched to scribble down a few.

Pete had turned quiet. He never liked it when Dylan Easterby's name came up. "Later," he said.

"Bye." But as Lexie turned the corner, she wished Pete had stayed with her. Because even with her super-sharp, see-in-the-dark, vestige-vampire vision, she couldn't exactly believe what she was seeing. She had to blink. Rub her eyes. Look at her feet, count backward in Japanese, *shi, san, ni, ichi,* and look up again.

Nope. Her eyeballs didn't lie. Their building had been painted.

And not just any color. All five stories were now a violent and disturbing shade of . . .

Pink.

4

BLIX AND MITZI

Pink? *Pink?* A bedroom color splashed all over the outside? It was like wearing your underpants on your head. What kind of crime was this? Who could do such a thing?

Lexie touched a finger to her front door. It was as if the whole townhouse had been poured over with stomachache medicine.

Right down to the pink gargoyles at the windows. And the pink lion-head door knocker.

All pink. Pink, pink, pink.

And was that pink glitter on the roof?

"'I know not who these mute folk are who share the unlit place with me.'" Lexie spoke the snip of poem by somber Yankee poet Robert Frost, though she already had her suspicions.

Before she had a chance to take out her phone and snap a pic of the pink house to send to her parents, who spent their afternoons walking dogs for their dog-walking business, Wander Wag, or in band practice with their band, the Dead Ringers, the front door flew open and a bubble-gum pink mummy ran out the door, nearly mowing Lexie down.

"Help! Help!" hollered the mummy. "They're pinking up everything! They'll pink you, too!"

Hudson's voice, Lexie realized, though her brother was barely recognizable, wrapped head to toe in pink toilet paper. He was now galloping down the street. Uh-oh, thought Lexie. It looked like Hud was going to get batty. Hudson changed into a bat only if the conditions were exquisitely dark and peaceful or incredibly panicky. And now he was freaked out.

Sure enough, by the end of the block, Hudson swooped into the air, transformed. Snips and scraps of toilet paper floated from the sky like an extra-absorbent early snow.

Lexie ran inside, her boots sliding on the pink glitter that covered the floor.

From upstairs came the sounds of giggles and whispers.

"What's happening here?" she called out.

"S'tahw gnineppah ereh?" shrilled a voice.

Backwardsian? Now Lexie knew, for sure. Those dreaded pixies had arrived.

"Come down now, pixies," she commanded. "Seixip, won nwod emoc!" Lexie had studied backwardsian in the Old World, and she was fairly fluent, except she sometimes messed up and spoke right to left.

In a blink, three pixies stood before her. The girl pix was all pink, with a floss of pink hair, thin pink wings, and strawberry pink lips. The boy pix was purple, with violet wing freckles and a spiky cowlick.

The third pixie was a foot and a half taller than the other two, and she was dressed in a rather hideous, throw-uppy shade of green.

"Blix," he introduced himself.

21

"Mitzi," chirped the little pink pixie.

"Spitzi," said the septic green pixie, who, on closer scrutiny, didn't look very pix at all.

"Ouch!" squeaked Spitzi—whom Lexie had recognized as an imposter—as Lexie twisted off her fake plastic ear.

Lexie sighed. "Maddy, why are you dressed like a pixie?"

"It's for Hallo-month, duh." Maddy grabbed for her ear. "I was inspired by our houseguests, Mitzi and Blix. They're so awesome, I turned pix. Though I personally prefer a gorier getup."

"Where'd they go?" Lexie twirled in a circle. Blix and Mitzi had sprung off. From the dining room came sounds of glass tinkling and pixie snickers.

"You were supposed to show them to their gilded cage. Why didn't you do that the second they arrived?" Orville had delivered a pix-holding cage to the house that morning. It had its very own swing bar and scratching post. According to Orville, a pix couldn't truly relax unless it was caged or in hiding.

"Yeah. I tried. But these pixies wanted a more open swing," explained Maddy as she followed Lexie into the dining room, where Blix and Mitzi, who'd shrunk themselves to half their size, now perched on the chandelier, swinging it so hard that its prisms were dropping *plop plip plunk* like crystal raindrops onto the dining table.

"Get off the chandelier, pixies!" Lexie commanded. "I'm not going to say it backwards. And change our house from pinkstone to brownstone before my friend comes over."

In response, the pixies giggled. Lexie fumed. She hated giggling in any form but especially pixie form because it sounded so devious.

Maddy tugged at her arm. "You're making it worse," she hissed. "Have you forgotten about pixies? Anger confuses them. Hudson asked Mitzi how to improve his mummy costume for Hallo-month, and that's when she turned him pink. She wanted to be helpful, but Hudson got upset, which made Mitzi turn more things pink. Like, the whole house."

Lexie took a steadying breath. "The Old World books will tell us how to calm them."

"Cupcakes work best," said Maddy. "I already looked it up. You can woo a pix with homemade butterscotch cupcakes, a soothing tune, flattery, and nectar. I don't think that our supermarket carries nectar. But cupcakes, praise, and singing are easy enough."

The last thing Lexie wanted to do, with Mina coming over any minute, was appease a pixie. But she didn't have much choice. And she liked to bake. She dashed out to the kitchen and began to throw together the ingredients for cupcakes.

"I'll help," said Maddy as she got out the butter, eggs, flour, salt, and butterscotch flavoring.

"And I'll check on the pixies," said Hudson, who'd returned to perch on the kitchen windowsill. "By the way,

I've been keeping my jigsaw puzzles in the oven. So careful before you preheat." Then he swooped off.

Lexie chucked the puzzles out of the oven and stuck in the cupcakes. Maddy mixed the frosting and licked up most of it.

"Update," reported Hudson, swooping back in. "First, the good news. The spell wore off, and our house is brown again. Now the bad news. The pixies are still swinging from the chandelier. Also, Mitzi asked me if you were mad."

"Obviously." Lexie snorted. "The most popular girl in my class is coming over any sec, and my home is a plague of persnickety pixies."

"Shh!" Maddy pressed a finger to her lips. "They've got better hearing than us. You need to flatter them, not diss them, remember?"

Lexie sighed. "Darling houseguest pixies!" she called out. "You enchant us with your shrill giggles!"

"You sound insincere," said Hudson. "You need to sell it, Lex. They knew when I was feeling anti-pix." He stared at his pink hands and sighed.

Lexie threw down her pot holders and stormed into the dining room. "Scrumptious pixies, you have brought light and laughter into our home," she began, and then, hands folded, recited: "'Come away, O human child! To the waters and the wild. With a faery, hand in hand, for the world's more full of weeping than you can understand.'" She took a little bow. "The Stolen Child" was one of her favorite poems by the pixie-sympathizing Irish poet William Butler Yeats.

From above, Blix stared down at her. His eyes clouded from glittering lavender to an angry indigo. "Me Blix no poems me hates."

"Sorry," said Lexie, trying not to sound hurt. What was up with this pix? His eyes swirled like kaleidoscopes. And did the eye swirling have anything to do with the itchy feeling between her shoulder blades?

A twitch, a shimmy, and a gravity-defying hop confirmed the worst—the pix had just spelled Lexie with a pair of flimsy, mothlike wings.

Briiing. Doorbell. Lexie jumped.

"You two keep praising the pixies," she commanded her siblings. "I'll answer that."

With a pounding heart, she fluttered out to the hall, pulling on her overcoat to hide her chintzy pix wings. It could only be one person: Mina.

Good-bye, brand-new friendship, thought Lexie. Hello, same old crushing embarrassment.

5

MAGIC RING

Darling, how're you—" Mina blinked. "Oookay, Lex. Why are you wearing a winter coat indoors?"

"I . . . I . . ."

"Are you hiding something?" Mina yanked off Lexie's overcoat. "Oh, honey, who knew you took ballet? And you're so clumsy, too! It must be quite a challenge. But you don't have to keep *that* a secret from me—look." Mina unbuttoned her own, adorable fall jacket to reveal that she herself was dressed in a peach leotard, peach tutu, peach tights, and silvery peach wings.

"I didn't have time to change out of my ballet clothes before coming over," Mina explained. "Friday afternoons, I study dance at Hansel Schumacher's studio. For me, the words *human* and *dancer* are always entwined." She smiled. "Inspiring thought, isn't it?"

"Uh-huh." Though Lexie was pretty sure that Mina was quoting that last sentence from her PHOLD. But she had replaced the word *poet* with *dancer.*

"Well, um, yes, I like dancing, too," she said. "Although I'm better at karate."

"I guess you're at a second-rate dancing school," said Mina, "because *everyone* who's *anyone* dances for Hansel.

26

Even Kaylee Milquetoast sees him, for VIP lessons. Oh! I didn't know you had other guests."

Mitzi and Blix had appeared. They'd managed to stretch themselves all the way to Maddy's height. Lexie had a hunch this was as tall as their pix tricks could take them, and it made them look overly narrow. She cringed. Even if their heights weren't suspicious, what would Mina think about their pastel skin? And their wings? And Blix's cowlick, pointing like a purple stalagmite off the top of his head?

"Hims Blix me Mitzi," said Mitzi. She squinted, looking Mina up and down, studying her peachy attire. "New World girls copycats pixies, yes?"

"I'm not sure what you mean," said Mina, giving the pixies a cautious once-over. "I'm part of Hansel Schumacher's troupe. But I think I've heard of the New World ballet studio. It's on Eighth Avenue in Chelsea, right? Are you in a pageant? I don't recognize your costumes."

"We're all in *A Midsummer Night's Dream*," bellowed the always-eavesdropping Maddy as she swept into the room with a plate of frosted cupcakes. "Hi, I'm Maddy, Lexie's kid sister, and these are my friends. We're rehearsing our parts for the ballet. We play the fairies."

"Ew, no way! Us hates stinky fairies," said Mitzi before Maddy stuffed a cupcake into her mouth.

"Our hallways are really long," continued Maddy. "They're perfect for grand jetés and pas des deux-es. Cupcake? They're homemade."

Lexie sent her sister an appreciative smile. Nice work, Mads.

"How sick that we all take ballet," chortled Mina, lifting a cupcake to her lips. "Mmm, thanks. Don't mind if I—"

"Hands off Blixie's yum!" Blix snatched the cupcake from Mina's hand and popped it in his mouth.

"Excuse me. You've got some horrible manners," said Mina. "You must be in middle school." She reached for another cupcake.

"No eat cutie Mitzi's snacky, greedy yellow-hairs troll!" Mitzi not only grabbed the second cupcake, she slapped Mina's hand, hard. Lexie winced.

"Ouch!" Mina blinked, shocked. "I'm not greedy! Or a troll! What school are you kids from? P.S. 114? P.S. 23?" Her eyes narrowed. "You do realize I'm in ninth grade, don't you?"

"Actually, my friends are from, um, Butterscratch, which is really far away," said Maddy. "They're here on ballet scholarships. And the only thing they eat in Butterscratch is brown rice and Vitaminwater. So of course they're excited to taste something as delicious as a cupcake."

"Yes, yes," added Lexie. "Please forgive how rude Blix and Mitzi are. They hardly know English, plus they're jumpy from eating sugar."

"Also, the word *troll* means 'doll' in Butterscratchian," explained Maddy. "So what might sound like an insult is actually a compliment."

"Ah," said Mina. "That makes sense. Everyone says I look like a doll with my curls."

"Say, Maddy, could you take your friends upstairs?"

Lexie was getting desperate. The piggy pixies were stuffing cupcakes into their mouths as fast as they could.

The treat did seem to be working its magic, though. With every tasty gulp and swallow, the pixies calmed down.

Then Mitzi burped. Blix passed a squeak of gas. Both of them rubbed their full stomachs and licked up the last of the cupcake crumbs.

The others went silent with horrified wonder.

"Dance now!" crowed Blix, snapping his spindly fingers.

"Loves it, Blix!" sang Mitzi. "Us dance the Wiley Eye Rabbit."

Without further ado, they clicked on the Livingstones' sound system, snatched up the other girls' hands, and swung them all into a Mitzi-Maddy-Mina-Blix-Lexie-back-to-Mitzi circle.

Whirling and twirling.

Swirling and skipping.

"Hey, the Wiley Eye Rabbit is fabulous!" enthused Mina. "And you're so light on your feet, maybe you should audition for Hansel Schumacher. Well, not you, Lex. Wheee!" She made a parrot-squawking noise.

Lexie wished she wasn't such a klutz. Even in this simple dance, her long feet kicked like clunky cinder blocks. She hoped that when she shed the last of her vampirishness, she'd inherit some grace.

The Wiley Eye Rabbit wasn't hard, but it was fast, and the pixies kept upping the tempo. And soon Mina, the only fullblood human in the dance, began to tire.

"Okay, okay, time-out," she huffed. "I need to rest."
But the pixies wouldn't stop. They were singing a strange
tune that had no words, only foghorn sounds, with some
giggling thrown in.

Uh-oh. Warning. I think this is a fairy ring, Maddy bounced
to Lexie. *You can't break free, can you?*

A fairy ring? Oh, noooooo. Lexie struggled to unlatch
her left hand from Mitzi's. No luck. Then her right hand
from Blix's. No dice. It was as if both of her hands had
been coated with superglue.

Just like "The Stolen Child" poem, thought Lex. But
in that poem, the phrase "a faery, hand in hand" had
sounded charming and quaint.

The reality was a nightmare.

Can't get free. I'm totally stuck, she bounced.

The oldest trick in the Old World book, bounced Maddy.
*Dumb us. We could be locked up in this ring forever if we don't
hatch a plan.*

The threat was real. Pixies have absolutely no sense of
time, which is very dangerous, especially when a favorite
pix trick is to sneak a human into a fairy ring for an en-
chanted dance that can last from seven minutes to seven
years.

Quick, get Hudson! Lexie bounced. *He needs to crash
through the ring from the outside.*

I'm right here. Hudson had been watching all along,
sitting cross-legged on the mantelpiece. And he had his
own ideas.

I'll break the ring, on two conditions, he bounced. *First, from Maddy: I want to wear your green pixie costume for one day of Hallo-month. Second, from Lexie: I want you to bake another batch of butterscotch cupcakes, all for me.*

Okay, okay! bounce-chorused the girls.

And hurry! Lexie could see that Mina was losing it.

"I'm done with this dance." Mina was jerking and twisting, trying to break free. "Let me go. It's hurting my feet."

"Ha ha ha," shrieked Mitzi.

"No, I mean it," said Mina. "I'm all sweaty and my ankles are sore."

"Pixies dances your feets to bloody stumps!" croaked Blix.

"Are you insane?" Mina screeched. "What's wrong with you crazy kids?"

"Pixies dances till your hairs turns gray and your trolly eyeballs falls out," sneered Blix.

"I don't think they mean 'doll'!" cried Mina, turning to the others. "These Butterscratchers are so hostile. Why can't we stop dancing?" Her eyes dashed with tears. "Does anyone know the Butterscratch words for 'I am going to call the cops if you don't let me go this minute'?"

But by now, Hudson had swooped in between the linked hands of Mina and Maddy. Using all his strength, he shoved a firm foot into the middle of the ring, then shouted the de-spell: "Jump-stump-bump-thump, from magic ring to weary lump!" and rammed his full weight against the girls' locked hands.

The pixies wailed. Mitzi stomped on Hudson's foot.

"Yowch!" he cried as Mina's grasp slid from Maddy's and the dance collapsed into a shrieking pileup.

Lexie could feel her spell wings evaporate as she rolled away and looked around. Mina, gasping where she'd fallen, had curled up and closed her eyes. And Maddy, who easily got motion sickness, was green as boiled kale.

Hudson stood and hobbled off, muttering about an ice pack for his toe.

Finally, Blix and Mitzi scurried out of the room to find a cozy, private spot to rest. "Us sleepy," they muttered. Then, in true pixie fashion, they scrabbled under the warm radiator and turned themselves into hedgehogs. All you could see of them were their pink hedgehog noses.

Lexie glanced over at Mina, but she was still collecting herself, slowly standing up. One wing had torn off her ballerina costume, and her tulle was ripped and trailing.

She had no idea, thought Lexie, how lucky she was. If they'd truly been trapped in the magic ring, the next time Mina would have walked out of the Livingstones' house, she'd have been a full-grown, twenty-one-year-old adult.

But Mina didn't know that. "Um, Lexie?" she whispered.

"Yes?"

"I guess I'm not in the mood to do speechwriting anymore." Mina looked pooped. "Where are those awful Butterscratchers? I want to give them a piece of my mind. I feel like I just ran a marathon. My feet are throbbing."

"They went . . . to the store. Hey, maybe we can work on the speech tomorrow?" suggested Lexie. "At your place."

But Mina, grumbling, was already on her way out the front door.

There was only one person who could help Lexie with her pixie plight. Even if he'd most likely want to give Blix and Mitzi a high five for dancing Mina off her feet. "But maybe I don't have to mention Mina specifically," Lexie decided as she went off to find him.

6

THE LONELIEST NUMBER

Bad, bad, bad," said Pete as he and Lexie slurped their Garden of Diva smoothie. They were enjoying a mid-afternoon break at their favorite weekend hangout, the Candlewick Café. The smoothie was made from banana, soy, cucumber juice, honey, cinnamon, and a pinch of bee pollen. "A pixie influx in your house can be a big problem. They used to drive my mom and dad bonkers back in the Old World."

"What would your parents do to control them?" asked Lexie.

"Well, they bribed them with cupcakes, of course. And they left ragwort branches in the corners for the pixies to jump on and, hopefully, fly away on—ragwort is like a Porsche to a pix. And they tunneled pix holes for them in case they wanted to leave by ground."

"The problem is, we can't drive them out. We're hosting them," Lexie explained.

"You need to keep them happy, or they'll make you miserable. One thing they like is . . ." Pete's voice trailed off as he checked his text messages.

"Is *what*?" Lexie sat back. Pete had been way over-checking his texts during smoothie time.

"Is . . . ah . . . walnuts . . ." Pete's fingers were a blur. He smiled down at his screen. A private-joke type of smile.

Lexie banged the table. Smoothie goo spattered.

"What?" Pete blinked.

"Pete, this whole time you've been speaking to me with half your brain and using the other half to text. To be honest, I don't think you've got enough mental power for both activities." Lexie snatched his phone and looked in on his conversation.

"Who is *Crunchee*?"

"Give that back!" Pete blushed. "She's my friend. We met at a Save the Chimps convention."

"I didn't know chimps needed to be saved." Or that Pete blushed. Or had a secret friend.

"Well, they do, and I'm helping save them," said Pete, grabbing back his phone. "I'm also meeting Crunchee later on at a Save the Dolphins rally downtown." He paused. "You could come along."

"Three's a crowd," said Lexie lightly. Though she did want to help save dolphins, she mostly wanted Pete to tell her that it was Crunchee, not her, who'd turn three into a crowd. She sat back and waited for him to say this.

"Suit yourself," said Pete.

Lexie's fangs itched in surprise. So Pete didn't want her to come. Had that ever happened before? "Maybe Mina and I could go to the rally together, and we could all meet up," she suggested, just to remind Pete that he wasn't her only friend. "I'm sure Crunchee would like Mina."

35

"I'm sure not. Mina's a dung beetle, and Crunchee's adorable."

Another surprise. Lexie couldn't remember the last time Pete had used the word *adorable*.

Except Pete used to think I was adorable, she reminded herself. Did he still?

They paid the check and parted ways. It was Saturday, and once Pete had deserted her for dolphins and Crunchee, left-behind Lexie didn't have much else to do. Maybe she'd put the last touches on Mina's notes for Monday's speech. Then she could just walk it over to the Pringle apartment to drop it off.

No big deal.

And if Mina was home and offering peach bars—well, that would be an awesome bonus. Lexie hadn't seen or heard from Mina since yesterday's pixie escapade. She hoped her new friend wasn't holding a grudge.

Lexie dashed back to her house, then tiptoed inside. She didn't want to wake Blix and Mitzi, in case they were napping. Unfortunately, they were both awake, shrunk down to their plumpest, shortest selves, and hanging upside down from the swing bar of their gilded cage, where they were reading *Learning New World Slang*.

As soon as they saw Lexie, though, they began to whine. "Make cupcakes, please, Sweet Cheeks!"

"Here," said Lexie, throwing them a bag of walnuts instead.

"Eeee!" They ripped open the bag and began to devour the contents.

Lexie shuddered. She'd forgotten how the elf-pix-fairy kingdom could crack nutshells by jacking them under their brittle armpits and then pick out the meat with their triangle teeth.

"O Punkin," crooned Mitzi, spitting out walnut as her eyes lit on Lexie. "Me still hungry needs to go to market, to market."

"I doubt you're starving, Mitz," said Lexie. "Considering you and Blix have each eaten one dozen homemade cupcakes apiece since morning and now you've almost finished that whole bag of walnuts."

"O Lex with the honey voice," chimed in Blix, "carry poor Blixipoo to Central Park?"

"I'm sorry, I can't," said Lex. "Maybe you could turn into hedgehogs and take a nap or something."

Which made the pixies jump right-side up and throw walnut shells at her. Lexie sighed and ducked. She'd forgotten. No matter how many times they're told, pixies don't believe that they can turn into hedgehogs when they sleep.

It had just been so long since she'd dealt with pixies.

"Ouch ouch ouch." The shells hurt. Lexie ducked them and rushed up the stairs.

She didn't want to be insensitive. But a pix in the park? Please.

"And if those pixies escaped on my watch, they'd be nothing but trouble to the New World. Orville would dock one of my human privileges for sure. Like appearing in mirrors and photos," Lexie thought out loud as she logged on to her laptop.

It was only last month that the Argos had bequeathed Lexie the honor of showing up in mirrors and photos. She had celebrated by moving all the mirrors in the house into her own room so that she could see herself from every angle. She'd come to the conclusion that while she wasn't gorgeous like Hudson or sassy like Maddy, she definitely had "eyes, like the Sherry in the Glass" as her favorite doomed poet, Emily Dickinson, had once poetically described her own.

Did Dylan Easterby appreciate her soulful sherry eyes? She knew he admired her double-jointed karate kicks. Last spring, when he'd sprained his ankle, Lexie had been the one to pick him up and carry him all the way to the emergency room. That had been a soulful moment, and Dylan hadn't been one bit intimidated by Lexie's strength. "You must be part bionic," he'd remarked, his voice filled with admiration as she strode through the hospital doors.

Being strong and soulful was one thing. Being pert and perky like Mina was another. And why did she have a nagging suspicion that even Dylan himself didn't know exactly which type of girl he preferred?

"*Bonjour*, Lexington." She blew a kiss to her thirteen reflections, who all *bonjour*ed and kissed her back. This made her feel a bit better as she pulled up her *M. Pringle Speech Points* document.

"Me has pixie prezzies for Lex," squealed Mitzi from downstairs. "Dlog, sdnomaid, revlis, dna selkcip!"

"No, thanks. I'm busy now," Lexie yelled back. She pressed the Print key.

From below, the conspiring pixies snickered. Blix and Mitzi possessed way too much energy for just one house, thought Lexie. And they had no idea how to channel it into anything useful. When she stepped out to the hall-closet printer, she learned their latest trick.

Mitzi had changed the printing-paper color from white to pink, and Blix had switched the print ink from black to purple.

"You two are super-annoying," she told them.

"Us only wanted to help," said Mitzi.

"Hunger pains makes us extra-mischievous," added Blix.

So Lexie relented and whipped up a couple of batches of butterscotch cupcakes before she left.

"Sweetie-punkin Lex really loves her pixies," Mitzi crooned as Blix hummed between bites.

"Yeah, yeah." She was out the door before she had to hear more pix nonsense. How long would Blix and Mitzi be here? Orville hadn't exactly answered this question when he'd stopped by yesterday. Sure, he'd been a help. He'd coaxed the pixies back to their cage, but only after they'd made a mess of the entire house, shredding curtains, throwing pots and pans all over the kitchen, and drawing tasteless pictures on the walls with their glitter pens.

"They're bored. Pixies need jobs," Orville had explained. He'd also assured the worried Livingstones that they'd be leaving soon, soon, soon.

"But who could *want* these berserk creatures?" Lexie's mother had asked.

"The Argos think they've found employment for them at an inn," Orville had answered. "Every country inn—even in the New World—likes to have a couple of pixies, even if they occasionally sour the milk and scare the cat. But they can be an advantage, too—they plant incredible varieties of wildflower, and people love to hear them whistle at dawn. Many people think that an inn isn't truly authentic without pixies.

"Meantime, never let them sing a lullaby to you." Orville shook his head in emphasis. "Once they lull you, you're putty in their hands. And nobody ever wants to be pixie putty."

Definitely not me, Lexie agreed silently as she slipped out the door.

7

A DIRTY TRICK

If it isn't the skinny speechwriter. Mina loves to quote you, by the way," Nina Pringle said as she let Lexie inside. "I'm on the campaign, too. I'm a gofer. It's not bad. My sister's paid more attention to me all week than this entire year."

"That's nice." Lexie looked around. "Where is she?"

"On the patio with her boyfriend. This way."

Boyfriend? Lexie's heart pounded with fresh worry. Her shiver of misgiving turned to a freeze of shock when she saw Dylan Easterby lounging on a patio chair. It *was* Dylan, wasn't it? He had mud smeared all over his face and a cucumber slice covering each eye.

"Nice to see ya, Lex," said Mina in her special, flirting-with-Dylan voice. "Take that table in the far corner— no, the one even farther—and set up a study nook for yourself." She clapped. "Nina!"

"Am I finished with my facial?" asked Dylan through his mud-cracked lips as Nina appeared with folders, pens, index cards, and a plate of peach bars.

"Not yet," crooned Mina.

Lexie took a peach bar. "Dylan, are you working on Mina's campaign, too?"

41

"No, darling," Mina said before he could answer. "I'm giving Dylie Willie a spa treatment. I want spa treatments recognized as a Parrish community service. It's part of my campaign. Isn't that genius?"

"Lucky you, Dylie Willie," Lexie teased. "I don't think I've ever seen you wearing vegetables before."

"First time for everything." An embarrassed Dylan had already peeled off the cucumbers. "Arright, Mina, thanks for the . . ."

"Deluxe rejuvenating facial, with a stimulating grape-seed-infused mud buff." Mina smiled. "Dylie pepper, you deserve some tender loving care."

"Yeah, okay. But what I really wanted to talk about was the soccer team. We lost our last three games, and kids' spirits are down. Can you give me more of the pep talk that you put in your last note? You've really got a way with words."

Lexie bristled. "Mina's got a way with *my* words, you mean," she said. "Otherwise why would she need a speechwriter?"

"Down, girl." Mina wrinkled her nose at Lexie as she hopped out of her seat. "And true inspiration comes from here." She patted her heart. "One sec." She dashed out of the room and returned with a slip of paper. "Here's a little poem I wrote called 'Everyday Victory,'" she said with a glance at Lexie. Then, in a hushed voice, she began: "'If you're feeling down and out and glory's passed you by, listen to this winning plan and then give it a try.'"

Lexie couldn't believe what her supersonic vampire ears were hearing. She clenched her fingers around her pen. Those words were from her poem "Ode to My Feet." She'd written it to make herself feel better about her long banana feet. Mina must have stolen the poem from Lexie's PHOLD and changed the words.

"'Cut back complaints, stay tough, don't whine. A silver trophy's quite divine,'" recited Mina.

Lexie fumed, though she also had to hand it to Mina. While the original words had been, "Cut back hangnails, buff, and shine. Leave icky tortoise toes behind," Mina's remake wasn't bad.

Not bad, but not fair. And poor Dylan had no clue that he was listening to copied inspiration. "Awesome." He whistled through his teeth.

"Oh, please. It's just a little gloppy poem I wrote." Mina snuggled up right next to him on the lounge, tossing aside the paper. Lexie fumed. *A little gloppy poem?* Why, that ode had taken Lexie days to make perfect.

"A wise man once said that 'he that readeth good writers and pickes out their flowres for his own nose is lyke a foole,'" Lexie quoted. She could hear the anger squiggling in her voice.

"Honey, you're trying too hard." Mina snickered. "Don't force the muse. You need to relax."

And *you* need a good bite on the neck, thought Lexie.

"What's wrong, speechwriter?" asked Nina. "You look paler than usual—if that's possible. Why aren't you working on a speech for my sister?"

43

"Bathroom first." Lexie slipped inside and ran to Mina's bedroom instead.

It didn't take long to discover what she was looking for. Just as she thought. Sneaky Mina had ripped out several pages of Lexie's PHOLD. They made a packet under her history book, with many of Lexie's words crossed out and Mina's bubble writing added in. Of particular horror, Lexie's tribute poem to her favorite doomed post-punk band, Joy Division, had become a tribute to Kaylee Milquetoast.

"That's a cosmic insult," Lexie mumbled as she smoothed out her precious papers, then slipped them into her folder. So, so wrong. What kind of a crooked politician was Wil-helmina Pringle if she had no guilt stealing somebody else's ideas for her own benefit?

That sappy smile and semi-snuggle that Dylan was giving Mina on the patio should have been for her.

"You were using me, same as ever," Lexie told the seashell-framed photograph of Mina. "I'll never be in your crowd unless you want something from me. That's the way it's always been, and that's the way it will always be, time unending."

She returned to the patio and tried to sound unbothered as she announced she was going home.

"Good idea," said Nina. "You look contagious."

"Bye, honey. See ya Monday." Mina spooned in closer to Dylan. She didn't even ask for Lexie's pink-and-purple papers. Just as well, since Lexie had decided right that moment to quit Mina's campaign.

She was shocked. She was outraged. She was through.

This time, Lexie didn't bother waiting for the elevator. She used her vamp strength to vault the fire-escape stairs, one entire staircase at a time. She was out on the street in seconds, her legs pounding the pavement in quarter-block leaps, so fast that other people jumped out of her way, yelling: "Watch it, Speedy!" and, "Where's the fire?"

Lex didn't care. The harder she ran, the madder she got. Where was the justice for someone like word-poaching, fake-friending Mina? To steal from her PHOLD was bad enough. But to steal from it so that she could entice Dylan? Outrageous.

Back at home, the pixies were confused to see Lexie's tears.

"Boooo hoooo! What is wrong with half-vampire girl?" bleated Mitzi.

"Hoooo hooo hooo! She is a chicken who is scared of chickens!" added Blix.

"I'm not scared of chickens, and I'm way less than half vamp," said Lexie. "I'll give you pixies another lesson in New World slang after dinner. Calling someone a 'chicken' doesn't mean you're saying that they're scared of chickens. I'm not scared of poultry. In fact, I have heartfelt reasons for crying."

"Heartfelt reasons?" Blix thought. "Or her means . . . fartsmelt raisins?"

Mitzi convulsed with laughter. "Tlemstraf snisiar!"

"What's wrong with you two-faced pixies? I make you

45

cupcakes, and you insult me. Thanks a lot." Lexie fled upstairs.

The pixies' voices screeched after her.

"Stay and play with us!" they called. "Us will be one faces, promise."

"Some other time!" Lexie slammed her door, then slammed her lavender-scented pillow over her head to muffle the pixies' voices telling Lexie that she was a farts-melt raisin chicken.

After a while, though, their words began to seep in and take on a new meaning.

Because I *am* kind of a chicken, Lexie thought as she replaced her loose PHOLD pages and set the restored book on her shelf. I've got thirteen PHOLDs, and none of them has translated into a single plan of action. What good is a philosophy if it can't turn into policy? What use is an opinion if it's never voiced?

Dylan liked Mina because she was a leader, not a follower. Mina always said what she thought and did what she wanted with a toss of her curly head and no care for the consequences.

But Dylan paid attention to Lexie when she acted like herself, too.

Like the time she scaled the wall to his apartment building. Or when she gave an impromptu guitar recital at lunch. Or when she read her "Elegy to Fun K. Blood" over the school's loudspeaker system. Maybe those weren't "cool" things. But they got Dylan's attention. In a good way.

I did it before, and I can do it again, Lexie thought. I've been going about this all wrong.

Why be a mere speechwriter, letting unworthy Mina take the credit and the glory, when I could be so much more?

When I could be, say, ninth-grade class president?

8

SPOILER

Listen up, family. Maddy and I are famous," Hudson announced at dinner that Monday. He was still dressed in Maddy's green Spitzi the Pixie outfit. Like anything and everything that Hudson put on, he looked gorgeous in it because Hudson was extremely handsome. "Almost famous, anyway."

"True, true." Maddy flashed a full-on, fangs-out grin. "We're going to be Livingstone legends." She was dressed as Doctor Death, in ketchup-spattered hospital scrubs and a stethoscope. Doctor Death was a variant on her Nurse Hatchet costume, which Maddy had considered a big-time success.

All day, Maddy had been swinging around her stethoscope and calling out her new catchphrase: "Dr. Death says, 'Have a heart-stopping Halloween.'"

"Explain, please. Why are you two legends?" asked their mother.

"Hallo-month," answered Maddy and Hudson together.

"See, we're turning Hallo-month into a celebration extravaganza," explained Maddy. "Everyone in Hudson's and my grades are so into our costume countdown. They've correctly pegged us as Halloween experts."

48

"Yeah, and if they knew that we're part vampire, too, they'd *really* call us experts," added Hudson.

"*Ex*-vampires," reminded Lexie.

"Whatever." Hudson continued, "Kids at school want us to create a haunted house for Halloween. We're going to do it—and it'll be totally eco-friendly, too. We'll have soy candles, no plastics, vintage costumes, local pumpk—"

"Yeah, and we're going to charge a dollar at the door," interrupted Maddy, "so we're guaranteed to make millions. Or twenty bucks apiece, at least."

"Also, old Madame Peabody from down the street said she'd help us with the spook factor," said Hudson. "Since she's got one of the creepiest houses in the neighborhood."

Lexie's parents nodded. Madame Peabody lived in a frightfully tall, narrow, crickity old house at the end of the block, and Madame herself was as hunched up and frizzle-haired as a witch.

"Sounds like you've got a perfect plan," said their father.

"So you'll let us? Can we do a spooky, brilliant, completely green haunted house here?" asked Hudson.

"Please please please?" Maddy spoke into her stethoscope for emphasis. "It'd be such a Hallo-hoot!"

Their parents exchanged a parental look. "It would be nice to get to know the neighbors better," mentioned their father. "Madame Peabody seems like a sweet old biddy."

"I agree. You can do it on two conditions," decided their mother. "First. New World rules only."

"Right. In other words," said their father, "you'd have to keep your vampire skills and thrills out of it."

"Second," continued their mother. "No candy apples. Smothering an apple in concrete-hard candy is a crime against fruit."

"How about some festive Mexican food?" suggested their father. "A little spice takes the sting out of a scare."

"Yeah, sure," said Maddy and Hudson, their voices sweet enough to make Lexie feel deeply doubtful.

"Kids at my school are too busy with elections to care about Halloween," she said, hoping to change the subject.

"Kids at our school are busy with Hallo-month," Hudson said. "For example, Mad's and my class got together and chalked a wall calendar in the front hall. It's called 'Thirty-one Tricks of October.' Everyone shared their favorite pranks, one for each day." He began to count them off. "How to short-sheet a bed, how to wedge a bucket of water over a door, how to put shaving cream on a toilet seat—"

"How to poison a vampire," chimed in Maddy, "how to make a box of disgusting, how to roll back your eyelids so you look like a zombie, how to—"

"Okay, okay, we get the idea," said their mother.

"At my school, we're outlining policy plans," said Lexie.

"Ooh, I hope the pixies are still here for Halloween," continued Maddy, as if Lexie hadn't spoken. "They know good tricks. This morning, Blix spelled a hairy wart onto my chin. Which was fine by me since it looked awesome with my Doctor Death costume. My chin didn't de-wart till lunchtime. That's good magic, eh?"

In the front hall, the pixies began to jabber proudly.

Their father shook his head. "No magic is good magic." Then he whispered, "And I, for one, will be happy when we're pix free."

The eavesdropping pixies rattled the bars of the cage and swore.

"Guess what? I'm running for class president," Lexie announced loudly. She was tired of trying to nudge the talk off Hallo-month. If she didn't force it, her siblings would chatter about their dumb haunted house forever.

"How wonderful, dear!" exclaimed her mother.

"What made you decide to do that?" asked her father.

Lexie reddened. She didn't want to say that her crush on Dylan or wanting revenge on Mina had motivated her.

"Government is interesting," Lexie said. Neil Needleburger had said that once.

But her answer didn't inspire any follow-up, election-related questions.

Their father stood to clear plates. "Whose turn is it to feed our guests?"

"Mine," said Lexie. It was always her turn. The pixies refused to take food from anyone else. She went to the kitchen to frost her latest batch of cupcakes.

Hudson and Maddy can brag all they want about their costumes and their haunted house, thought Lexie. I'll be famous in my own right. What she had requested earlier today was *unprecedented*. Mr. Fellows had even told her so.

• • •

"You're putting me in a sticky spot, Lexington." Mr. Fellows had clasped his hands while tapping the heels of his shoes together. "It's *unprecedented* for you to join the class presidential race at this late date."

"I'm a dark-horse candidate," Lexie had replied. "That means political intrigue."

"True." Mr. Fellows had looked down at his glossy shoe tips. "Tell you what. Prepare me an essay on what it means to be a great president and put it on my desk tomorrow." He raised his finger. "Something intriguing, okay?"

"Thanks, Mr. Fellows. I will." What she couldn't tell Mr. Fellows was that she'd lived through four centuries of political intrigue. She'd seen bloody coups, coldhearted assassinations, and passionate mutinies. She'd write that essay so well that Mr. Fellows would let her read it out loud for the class—including Dylan. "You won't be disappointed," Lexie promised her teacher.

She was glad that Mr. Fellows occasionally bent the rules. Of course, he himself was an intriguing person. For example, he owned over one hundred pairs of shoes. Some were antiques that he'd found in attics and yard sales. Others he had cut and stitched himself.

"Shoe cobbling is my avocation," Mr. Fellows had explained last month during Something About Your Teacher Day, when all the teachers at Parrish sat on the stage and explained little-known tidbits about themselves. "An avocation is the thing you love to do besides your job."

"Maybe politics is my avocation," Lexie thought out loud as she prepared her one-pager. Or, when she looked a little deeper, was her true avocation revenge?

Either way, Mina was in big trouble now. Nobody was going to rip off Lexie's PHOLD, then recite her own poetry back to her one true love and get away with it.

"'Ay, now by all the bitter tears that I have shed for thee, the racking doubts, the burning fears, avenged they well may be,'" she quoted to herself. Nothing sounded better in her own ears than these words of revenge-specialist poetess Letitia Elizabeth Landon, who was doomed to die from an overdose of cyanide.

• • •

First thing the next morning, Lexie dropped off her essay with Mr. Fellows. From the gleam in his eye when she walked into class, she knew her passionate words had sealed it.

But he didn't let her read it out loud. Another missed chance to show off for Dylan. Oh, well. There'd be others. After all, I'm a public figure now, she reminded herself. I'm a political candidate.

"Class, I'm pleased to tell you that Lexie is joining the race for ninth-grade class president," said Mr. Fellows with a small click of his tassel-tie loafers. "I'm pushing back the final speeches to the end of next week. We'll cast our votes on Halloween, and I'm hoping for one hundred percent turnout. Voting is one of our great democratic privileges.

To paraphrase a past president, 'A person without a vote is a person without protection.'"

Vote quotes! Lexie perked up as she remembered another one. "Also, 'Bad officials are elected by good citizens who do not vote!'"

"Say it loud, Lex!" Dylan clapped, although the other kids groaned. "Now this is getting interesting," he said.

"Now we *know* Mr. Fellows is crazy, from head to shoes." Mina's voice was easy to hear. "Nobody wants a pasty poetess for president."

"Except someone has to save us from turning this place into the Parrish Day Spa," said Lexie. "What's next if you're elected, Mina? Principal Kaylee Milquetoast?"

Mina buttoned up and didn't pounce again until lunchtime. Lexie and Pete were sitting outside, although that nip in the air had become a true bite.

"Hard to believe that once I lived on an all-blood diet of field mice and voles," Lexie mentioned as she spat apple seeds into her hand. "Seems so unhealthy."

"Or that I attacked my prey under a full moon," countered Pete.

They smiled a friends-with-a-secret smile. Pete wasn't texting anybody, and Lexie hadn't brought up Crunchee, so everything seemed good.

"Yucktopus Fingers! You're making a major mistake." Mina had sneaked up from behind with Loo on her side. Now she got right up in Lexie's face.

Lexie hated hearing Mina's old nickname for her. She

also hated hearing Loo's I-love-everything-about-Mina snigger.

"Not as big a mistake as the ones your parents made." Pete loved a good fight. His yellow eyes sparkled.

"Stay out of this, Stubbe. This is between me and my turncoat speechwriter." Mina's voice was so loud that other kids were tuning in. Lexie had to put down her apple because her nervous hand was slipping on the skin.

"The disloyalty started with you, Mina," Lexie answered. "You've been plundering my PHOLD for all your best inspirational lines."

But Mina waved the words away. "Fair use," she said. "If I get elected president, I'm in charge of freshman morale. Which means pep talks. Since, at the time, you *were* my speechwriter, I was using your words as *policy.*"

"Well, steal your policy from somebody else," Lexie said. "As of this morning, you're my opponent."

"Good. Fine. Nothing gets me going better than squashing losers like bugs," Mina sniffed. "Go ahead and run against me, *honey.* But all that happens now is that you and Needleburger will split the nerd-and-dork vote. That leaves me with the class majority: the jocks, the perfects, the cling-ons, the suck-ups, the thesps, the hippy dips, the bandsters, the rebs, the techies, and the burnouts." She wriggled ten fingers in the air.

"What am I?" asked Loo.

Mina rolled her eyes. "Mostly perf, with teensy elements of cling-on and suck-up."

Loo nodded. "You're so smart, Mina."

"Not smart enough," Lexie spoke up. "I'm going to win this election by a landslide, Mina Pringle, because your policies are as empty as a lost sock."

Mina sniggered. "How poetic. News flash—it's not the policies, it's the strategy. I've got this in the bag, Ape Feet. Say good-bye to the best chance you had to be cool by association. Now you can go back to torturing us with your stinky quotes, your cracking ankles . . . and don't even get me started on your green blood. My suggestion? Save yourself some heartache and get back to your own planet. Where you belong." With a bounce of her curls, she turned on her heel, Loo bopping along behind.

"Oof." Pete shook his head. "How does Mina know about your blood?" It was an insider secret that hybrid-vampire "blood" was blue-green.

"When I pricked my finger last year to sign Dylan's cast . . ." Strangely, the very word *blood* had made Lexie dizzy. It had been many, many years, so she hardly recognized this sharp craving for a glass of warm blood with a full-bodied aftertaste.

And not just any blood. Mina's blood. Which likely had a hint of peach.

Lexie's fangs itched as she tried to block out the ancient desire. What a peculiar sensation after all these years. All this bickering and squabbling was firing up her old vamp instincts. And that probably was not a good thing. "You were right, Pete. It looks like Mina's a slug after all," she said. "You'll help me with my campaign to beat her, won't you?"

Pete squirmed, uncomfortable. "Sure. Not today, though. Today, I'm meeting Crunchee after school. We're going to a Save the Bay rally."

"Chimps, dolphins, now the bay. Why are you so interested in saving things all of a sudden?"

Pete looked sheepish. "Guess I'm kind of like your brother, Hudson. I want to get eco-educated. And I'd rather save than waste. It'd be cool if you came along. You could meet Crunchee. She's pretty awesome."

But Lexie didn't like to hear about Crunchee. "It'd be cooler if you helped your best friend in her time of need."

Pete looked baffled. "How can I help you?"

Lexie sighed, exasperated. "Frankly, I was just asking myself the same question." She hadn't meant to say this as rudely as it came out.

"Ouch," said Pete. "Know what, Lex? Sometimes you throw words around like rocks, and they hurt when they hit."

Lexie scowled. "So I take it you're not going to work on my campaign with me? You'd rather hang out with this Crunchee person?"

Pete went silent. Lexie waited. All Pete offered was a frown.

They were used to disagreements and the odd, all-out spat, but this one felt different. How could Pete not sense how worried she was to be up against Mina? Or how reckless it now seemed to her to have thrown herself into a presidential campaign that she had a good chance of losing?

Lexie smashed up her lunch bag and popped in her retainer, then jumped up. "So that's the way it is," she said, even as she crossed her fingers that Pete would tell her that wasn't the way it was at all, that he was just kidding, that Crunchee really wasn't so awesome, and that he'd be way more into saving Lexie's skin than the bay.

Instead, he winged his sandwich crust all the way across the park. Lexie's supersonic ears heard the same hungry FDR Drive dog yip his thanks.

"You'd go out of your way to help a stray dog before a real friend," she noted.

"Come on, Lexie," said Pete. "We could campaign for the cause with Crunchee and then work on your stuff."

"Sorry. I guess I don't like to waste stuff, either. Especially not my time." Lexie tried to toss her hair à la Mina. "It looks like I'll have to win this one alone."

9

SQUAWK!

aybe it was all those cupcakes she'd baked them. Or the fact that she'd let them read her *Collected Poetry of W. B. Yeats* and *Complete Works of Sir Walter Scott*. Or that she'd been tutoring them in their favorite subject, New World slang. But when Lexie came home from school that afternoon, she learned that Mitzi and Blix had launched their own campaign: a request to move into Lexie's room.

"Family election," their father announced after dinner, ripping up little pieces of paper as their mother passed around an urn for them to cast their votes.

"Four ayes, one nay," Maddy reported a minute later. "Sorry, Hex."

"This is *so* not a good idea," said Lexie. "I was only trying to be polite to them."

"We have to give the pixies a haven," said her mother as she picked up the empty cage. "Otherwise they cause trouble all day. Yesterday, they stole papers from the newspaper girl. The day before, they demagnetized the UPS guy's signature pad. And they scare pretty much anyone who knocks on our door."

"Plus, your room is the closest thing to nectar for

pixies," said Hudson. "It's so super-extra girlie flowery pink and purple."

"Face it, you've been a marvelous example for them, Lexie," said their father. "Somehow, you calm them."

"Us loves Lex!" squeaked the pixies, who were already flitting up the stairs. "Us loves her yums cupcakes and pretty voice and her room of lavender ginger spicy smellies."

"It's a known fact that Lexie has the most off-tune voice in vampire lore," said Maddy. "You pixies sure can kiss up."

"No, the pixies truly adore Lexington," said their father. "Like it or not."

"*Not*. This is emotional blackmail." Lexie followed and watched with a sinking heart as her parents set the pixie cage next to her dresser. "How can I concentrate on anything if I have to put up with pix nonsense?" The spells. The cursing. The walnut-shell throwing. It would drive her bonkers.

"Us pixies helps win Lexie's contest for queen of the world," said Blix.

"Not queen of the world. Ninth-grade class president," said Hudson. "And I doubt you crazy pixies know how to—ouch!" He ducked the flying walnut shells and left Lexie's room quick.

"Thanks, sweetie," whispered their mother. "Remember, it's temporary." The Livingstones tiptoed out Lexie's door, leaving her alone with Mitzi and Blix, who had moved Lexie's pillows from her bed to their cage and now were snuggled up in them, humming with happiness.

Lexie took out her laptop. She'd start by writing an ode to everything she loved about Parrish. That would motivate her to tackle her campaign speech.

But what rhymed with *Parrish*?

"*Marrish, scarrish, rarrish,*" she murmured. Not great.

What about Dylan? *Chillin', thrillin'* . . . Dylan Easterby was certainly one of the main reasons she loved Parrish.

Blix hummed. "Uoy era gnitteg ypeeeeels."

"Huh?" Lexie's eyes felt heavy. "What are you saying?"

"Nepo ruoy wodniw," sang Mitzi, "dna neht og ot peeeeels."

"Good idea." Lexie stood up to do something. Then she immediately forgot what she'd done, and she put her head down on her desk to rest. She was so tired all of a sudden.

• • •

When she picked her head back up again, her room was freezing cold and sunlight was streaming through. What kind of dream was this? Why was it daylight? Why was her window—

"Argh!" This was no dream. Lexie jumped up and shut the window, then pulled down the blinds. Autumn afternoons were one thing, but the strong dose of morning sun was too much for her sensitive skin. She was starting to get skin crusties. Quickly, Lexie smeared on some sunscreen. She'd need to keep covered up today. How had she fallen asleep at her desk?

Then she saw. The cage was empty. The pixies were gone.

"I've been spelled," Lexie whispered as last night flashed back. The pixies had lullabyed her—and she'd done the unspeakable. She'd listened and *obeyed*!

What had Mitzi said? Lexie mentally replayed the backwardsian. Then her eyes brimmed with tears. Now she remembered standing up and unlocking the window, then opening it.

Oh, no. But it wasn't her fault. She had been working late. Their humming had confused her.

"Mooooooooom! Daaad!" Lexie ran downstairs, hiccuping with fear.

"Hey, Lexie," said Maddy. "Check out my new catchphrase—murder hobbles in!" She and Hudson were in all-new costumes—Maddy as Gory Granny, in a ketchup-spattered dress and a gray wig, while Hudson was dressed in Maddy's Elf Scout uniform.

"I don't need a catchphrase," said Hudson. "My incredible good looks carry me."

"The pixies escaped," Lexie gasped through her hiccups.

"Wow, you mess things up *quick*, Lex," said Hudson. "They were in your care for, like, one night?"

"Not in my care. Just in my room." Lexie hiccuped.

"Where do you think they went?" asked their father.

"How should I know? They sleep-spelled me and escaped through the window," squeaked Lexie.

"Uh-oh, I wouldn't want to be the one to tell Orville," said Maddy. "He's going to flip his beak."

"Okay," said their mother. "No need to panic. They could use a little freedom. Let's not report to Orville yet.

Perhaps they only went to the Macy's Fall Sale. They've been talking about it for days. I'm sure they'll come back once they get hungry and find out how expensive store-bought cupcakes are in this city."

Lexie nodded. She knew the pixies had wanted to go try out some of their city slang. All week, they'd been practicing phrases like, "Is this a knockoff or a lemon?" and, "My dogs are barking."

"I'll bake a batch of cupcakes for when they get back," Lexie said as she reached for the mixing bowl.

"And if they're not back by night, then we'll report to Orville," her mother said.

• • •

At school, the competition had edged up a notch. Mina's campaign team had made a huge banner that read: MINA PRINGLE GIVES ME TINGLES!

"She gives me tingles, too," Lexie overheard Dylan tell his friends. "Mina made me a spearmint foot scrub that's great for sore soccer feet."

Lexie's heart tripped. Why hadn't she thought of that? She could make a fantastic foot scrub. Mina Pringle was always one-upping her.

At the lockers, Neil Needleburger caught her eye and sidled over. "Lexie, I think we should team up. You could run as my vice president, and then we'd hold on to our core support."

"'Some leaders are born women,'" quipped Lexie. "I

appreciate your offer, but I kind of want to aim as high as you."

"Except you don't even like politics," said Neil. "Everyone knows you're running against Mina because she and Dylan are going out and you're jealous."

"They're not going out!"

Neil shrugged. "She made him a homemade foot scrub."

"Anyone can make a foot scrub! It doesn't mean anything." Lexie banged shut her locker. Mina Pringle's campaign was working, all right. It sure was giving her tingles—mad tingles.

• • •

Walking home, Lexie admitted it to herself—her motivations were all upside down. She'd entered this race for two wrong reasons—to impress a boy and get back at a girl. Speechwriting didn't make her a politician. "But I know I can come up with better policies than changing our mascot or building a fountain," she said. "After I find the pixies, I'm going to focus on a clean, smart campaign platform."

But upstairs, a surprise awaited her. "What are you two doing here?" Mitzi and Blix were sitting on the edge of her bed, hands folded, smiling broadly.

"Us fly away. Now here," said Blix as Mitzi nodded.

"I see that. Well, I'm glad you came back. And thanks for cleaning my room."

Her bedroom was spotlessly tidy and smelled like honeysuckle. Every surface shone or glittered. It had never looked so pretty.

But the pixies couldn't hide the reason for their goofy grins. "Us went out to get the dirt!" they exclaimed, bouncing on the bed. "Ask about dirt!"

"Huh?" Lexie couldn't find a speck of dirt anywhere.

"The dirt on troll girl." Mitzi waved a slender scrapbook in front of Lexie, then just as quickly snatched it away.

"Let me see that!" Lexie recognized the embossed monogram *W.A.P.*—Wilhelmina A. Pringle.

So it was *that* kind of dirt. The pixies had become so fluent in New World slang. "Dirt" really meant secret, possibly harmful information about Mina.

"Promise cupcakes for a pix," said Blix.

"Then us shows Lexie," added Mitzi.

"Fine," she said. "Cupcakes are already made. Now show me."

With a smirk, Mitzi tossed the book to Lexie, who popped it open.

"Ooooooh . . ." Her eyes gobbled the images. Page after page showed photographs of Mina Pringle dressed in safari bird-watcher's gear, one sock up and one sock down, sweaty-faced, with a pair of binoculars looped around her neck.

In some pages, she was scoping out birds from a low branch or shrub. In others, she was high up in a tree, binoculars aimed.

In the last picture, Mina was dressed in a feathered parrot costume, complete with huge headdress and a matching smile on her face.

" 'I love the Florida peach-blossom parrot more than any other bird in the world, and I would follow it to the ends of the earth.' " Lexie read Mina's caption out loud. " 'What a great summer. Thank you, Longwood, Florida, branch of the International Bird-Watching Society. My IBS memories will never fade. Squawk! Over and out!'

"Wow!" Lexie closed the book. "How interesting. Mina lied and told us she'd gone to Paris, France, for the summer. Instead, she was geeking it up at bird-watcher camp." Lexie wondered why Mina would work so hard to cover up her activities. She must be super-insecure about her nerdy side, Lexie decided. Which was too bad—since bird-watching was a fantastic hobby.

"Us got the dirt!" crowed the pixies. "Now you goes public!" Then they jumped into their cage, curled up, fell asleep, and turned into hedgehogs.

Go public. It seemed so easy. Yet so devious. All Lexie had to do was blow up that last picture of Mina in her peach-blossom parrot costume and plaster it all over the school. She would expose Mina as a liar. And, worse, as uncool—something that Mina took great pains not to be.

I can't really do this, though, thought Lexie. It would be immature. And mean. And low. Too low. What would Dylan think?

"If I'm really careful, he doesn't have to find out," Lexie said to herself.

She looked down at her hands and was surprised to see a dark ink stain smeared across her palm. She'd squeezed her pen so hard that she'd broken it. Strange. She usually had her vamp strength in check.

Of course, she didn't usually have such vampish thoughts.

She did now.

10

TINGLE IN THE AIR

Look, look, everybody—in the science hall!"

Kids were yelling and running through classrooms to make sure others came out and saw the posters. Lexie, innocently at work on her math work sheet at her desk, didn't bother to join them. She knew what she'd done.

She waited a day. But then couldn't resist. Mina would win the election unless people could see who she really was—a hypocrite and a poem thief. The posters of Mina in her parrot costume at the International Bird-Watching Society were up on the walls of the school because kids deserved to know the real Mina Pringle.

Under the picture, Lexie had written:

> Mina Pringle says she went to
> Paris last summer.
> But she really spent her days with
> her International Bird-Watching
> Society buddies.
> What else could she be hiding?
> V Is for Vote 4 Lexie
> 4 9th-Grade Prez!

A smear campaign was low-down, dirty politics at its best. And, Lexie promised herself, she had played fair by the smear rules. She had been vicious. She had been underhanded. She'd used her vampire powers only a little bit and only because they seemed to be itching for her to use them. For example, she'd called on a few of the mice that lived in Parrish's kitchen walls to tear down some of Mina's posters last night, while the school was closed. No rodent would dare disobey a vampire's command. Even if Lexie was rusty in her animal-language skills, she knew the word for "destroy."

She'd also tripped Mina during this morning's fire drill. Okay, maybe that had been immature. But it had been an impulse thing, where Lexie used her infamous, instant double-jointed karate kick. But Mina needed to look clumsier, Lexie decided. Less leader-y.

Except that when Mina went flying, Dylan had caught Lexie's eye. He didn't say anything, but his face seemed to question her.

The Parrot Poster Prank was working best. Listening to the kids hooting in the halls, Lexie had to smile. From a revenge perspective, she decided, this might be the best day of her New World life.

Her favorite moment came later that afternoon, when she saw that somebody had Magic Markered the word GEEK before the word TINGLES on the MINA PRINGLE GIVES ME TINGLES banner.

I've destroyed her campaign, thought Lexie as she ate

lunch alone since Pete had fencing practice. And it feels so sweet.

If only she could banish that memory of Dylan's questioning eyes from her mind.

It didn't help that she was feeling a bit prickly and all-around achy. Probably heartburn. Last night, after she'd printed up her copies of Mina in her bird costume, Lexie had done the unthinkable and eaten a mosquito—just for the rush of that squeegee of blood.

But, she reasoned uneasily, revenge was a vampire thing. In the Old World, vampires were always swearing vengeance on this family or that village. In tapping her vengeful nature, Lexie edged closer to her more-vampish self. It was a bit scary to think about it.

I'll re-humanize after the election, she decided, crossing her heart. In my heart, I know I'm still the same old Lexie. But right now, I need to focus on victory.

"Troll girlie is crying hoo hoo hoo in hers bed," reported Blix later that afternoon. "Us spies in her window."

"Good. Keep spying." Lexie figured that if the pixies kept making mischief for Mina, they wouldn't bother anyone else. So her bedroom window was left conveniently cracked open. Now the pixies could stay or go as they pleased. Mostly, they stayed, cleaning Lexie's bedroom until it gleamed and making fun of how Mina had danced the Wiley Eye Rabbit (even though Lexie had danced it worse).

"You pixies dislike Mina more than I do," Lexie mentioned.

"Us hates cupcake-stealer pixie-pretender troll girl who called us insane!" screeched Mitzi, so loud that Lexie had to cover her ears.

• • •

Later that week, Mina surprised Lexie by making an announcement at the end of homeroom. "Hi, everyone. I just want to remind you that I'll be giving out crumble-top peach bars in the cafeteria today." She grinned as the classroom applauded. "One more thing. By now, all of you know I like bird-watching. Well, good. I want people to get to know every aspect of my character. In living your life, you should never be too timid and squeamish about your actions. All life is an experiment, and the more experiments you make, the better."

As she walked back to her seat, Mina actually had the nerve to look proud. But Lexie was horrified. Mina was quoting Ralph Waldo Emerson! And, once again, she wasn't attributing it. Nobody seemed to notice.

Lexie's vampire blood surged with aggression, and before she could stop herself, she'd jumped to the front of the room. "I also have something to say," she announced as she picked up a chair in one hand and, in a movement so fluid and expert it could not have been called human, balanced its back leg off the tip of her nose.

The class gasped. Mr. Fellows's jaw came unhinged. Right as Pete's best friend, Alex Chung, reached for his cell phone to snap a photo, Lexie let the chair fall.

71

"And that is, when electing your class president," she continued as she set the chair neatly in place behind its desk, "never, ever settle for ordinary."

No quotes, no poems. No photographic evidence. Just a wink and a small bow as Lexie headed back to her seat amid a murmur of amazement and scattered, awed applause.

She could feel her fangs scrape against her bottom gums, and her temperature had dropped to a chilly Old World level. The strength and balance of such a pure vampire antic had surely cost her human points. She could almost hear Orville sighing in despair.

The look on Mina's face was worth it.

• • •

The next day, with help from the pixies, Lexie had created another sign, this one made from gluing two photographs side by side. The first photo was of herself tending a cherry-tomato vine from her kitchen window box. Next to it was a photo of Mina, mouth open, eating a big, sloppy cheeseburger.

Underneath, she'd lettered:

Carnivore Pringle's policy is like
her lunch—dead on arrival.
BUT
Veggie-loving Livingstone will
nurture our school.
V Is 4 Vote 4 L.L.!

This caption wasn't quite true. Lexie had pixi-morphed the photo—which had originally been of Mina eating a cheese sandwich. But a greasy, dead-cow cheeseburger looked ickier against her gorgeous tomatoes.

It had been Blix who'd shown Lexie how to pixi-morph. One touch of his finger to the photo and he'd supplied Mina with a sweaty upper lip, a double chin, and a gross, greasy, gristly burger. The final image made Mina look like a pig *and* a slob.

Though Lexie had some doubts, the pixies' enthusiasm gave her confidence. It was just the usual campaign-prank stuff, after all.

"Nice work, Blix. You two are my stealth weapons," Lexie admitted to them that evening. "My sign was a hit."

The pixies twittered and threw some dust around, pinking and purpling Lexie's room as Lexie sat on her bed and tore the paper from her hamburger tartare that she'd ordered from Boeuf, a fancy French restaurant. It had wiped out her allowance, but her taste for raw meat had sharpened this week. All day at school, she'd day-dreamed of sinking her fangs into something other than fruits.

And the minute after I win the election, she promised herself, I'll resume my principled, vegetarian lifestyle.

The problem was, what was happening to her now? What was she doing, eating a pound of raw beef before dinner? I'm the same old Lexie, she reassured herself for the umpteenth time, but she wasn't sure she believed it.

73

• • •

Downstairs, Lex could hear her father preparing dinner, a mushroom-and-kale casserole that was his specialty. Eee-yew.

When she appeared for dinner, her mother scrutinized her. "You okay, Lex? You look a little glassy-eyed." She placed her hand on Lexie's forehead. "And you feel very cool. Make sure you double up on your irons, okay?"

"Sure." She reached for her cup of cranberry juice and pretended to sip.

"Do you think you'll be feeling good enough to come with Maddy and me to visit Madame Peabody's house on Thursday?" asked Hudson. "She told us she could give us some tips for our haunted house."

"And between the two of you," added Maddy, "we should have some bloodcurdling ideas."

Lexie frowned. "What do you mean, 'between the two of us'?"

Her little sister shrugged. "Just, 'cause Madame Peabody's so witchy and you're so sneaky. I've seen those campaign posters you and the pixies have been making."

From upstairs, the pixies screeched with pride.

Maddy was watching Lexie closely. "Are you wearing lipstick on your lips or is that blood?" she whispered.

Startled, Lexie wiped her mouth. "Cranberry juice," she muttered.

But Maddy's nose was twitching. "I didn't fall off the turnip truck yesterday," she hissed. "If you don't help us with the haunted house, I'm telling Mom and Dad that you're back on blood."

"Your threat falls on deaf ears," said Lexie. But she knew Maddy was serious. When it came to blackmail, Maddy was always serious.

Next Monday at school, Lexie floated through the halls, accepting smiles from kids who hadn't known who she was until this past week. "Heya, Lex! You got my vote." A burly guy gave her a high five as she passed. Burly Guy was in karate class with her. What was his name again?

"Mine too," said the gap-toothed girl standing next to him, flashing Lexie the victory sign. "That thing you did with the chair last week—truly awesome."

"Thanks . . ." As Lexie flashed her fingers in an extra-long *V*-for-victory sign, she made a mental note to brush up on names.

Another reason you're not a true politician, nagged her inner voice. You're bad with names.

"Hey, sexy Lexie. Guess what?" Dylan Easterby bounded up, smiling at Lexie as if she was his best friend.

Her heart immediately started doing the rumba. Did Dylan really think she was sexy? She tried to seem unfazed while at the same time look extra-sexy. "Okay, let me guess. You're voting for me, too?"

"More interesting. It looks like I'll be running against you. Mr. Fellows said it was unprecedented, but he's letting me. Let's face it—Mina's ditzy, and Neil's a snore."

"And I'm . . . ?"

Dylan's green eyes glinted. "You're more poet than politico."

Lexie arched an eyebrow, but what could she say? He was right, of course. "So what's your strategy?"

"I'm gonna inject some adrenaline into this race. I've got tons of ideas about how to improve our athletic department." He flashed his charming Dylan grin. "Maybe I'll even get karate approved as a spring sport. You'd like that, wouldn't ya? I saw you give a good kick the other day in fire drill."

"Oh . . . right." Lexie's mind spun. This was bad. First of all, how would Dylan be impressed with her victory if he himself wanted to win? Second, he was obviously on to her lame attack on Mina. "That's a smart platform, Dylan," she mustered.

"You bet. Just wanted to tell ya in person. Now I gotta find Needleburger. Oh—and may the best frosh win." Dylan gave Lexie a parting, good-natured jab in the ribs before he spun around to shoot an imaginary ball through an imaginary hoop. Then he turned back. "And Lex? I'm aiming to run an honest campaign. Just so you know, I'm not into tricks. On or off the field."

11

CHARACTER IS DESTINY?

With everyone so excited about our student election, I've allowed two more candidates to put their names on the ticket," announced Mr. Fellows the next morning. "Dylan Easterby and Riley Burnett. And now I have officially closed the ballot. No more nominees. Five's plenty."

Riley Burnett?

All heads in the class turned. Riley was new this year. She was the kind of girl who hardly talked, with the kind of face people hardly remembered.

Lexie was shocked. Poor Riley. Who would vote for that mute mouse? If she and Pete were on friendlier terms, they'd have laughed about it. Meantime, thought Lexie, the pixies surely can scoop me some dirt on Riley.

That is, if I even need it.

As of yesterday, according to Jasmine Lee—who loved statistics and probabilities—Lexie was in the lead to win. Jasmine announced it in the cafeteria, and by the end of lunch Mina's friend, Loo Suskind, had sidled up to her.

"I bought you a cup of pudding," said Loo. "Caramel."

"Oh, thanks." Lexie was delighted. She loved caramel pudding.

Loo handed her a spoon and a napkin. She sat quietly

as Lexie spooned up the dessert. "Jasmine says you've got a good chance to win," Loo mentioned quietly, "and I just want to say I always saw you as a really edgy goth girl. Also, I don't think your feet and fingers are too long like Mina always says."

"Thanks." Lexie wiped her mouth. Loo was fantastic at sucking up. It was kind of amazing and embarrassing.

"Another thing," continued Loo, "if you get elected, I hope you'll appoint me to social chair. I'd be awesome at it. All I think about is socializing. As Mr. Fellows might say, being social is my avocation."

"I'll remember that," murmured Lexie, staring at her empty cup of pudding, which she now saw for what it was—a political bribe.

"Cool! Then I'll put out the word—vote for Lex!" exclaimed Loo, flashing her best socialite, high-wattage smile. "Our only real problem is Dylan. But you'll scoop something on him, right?"

"Sure." Inwardly, Lexie quaked. Was that how Loo saw her, as a campaign sneak? She hurried home after school in a cloud of troubled thoughts.

And was Loo right? Would she have to get dirt on Dylan? What a depressing idea. The truth was, Lexie already knew the dirt on her longtime crush because she'd had her eye on him for years. Dylan couldn't do karate, for one thing—though he practiced every night in his underwear. He was also bad at history, and every time one of his quizzes or papers came back, he mashed it into the bottom of his book bag. Also, his little brother, Charlie, could beat him in an arm-wrestling contest.

Using this private information against her love seemed horribly heartless. This election was turning her conscience upside down. How could she impress Dylan and at the same time derail him? It defeated the whole purpose of the campaign.

Lexie gave a hop of frustration and was surprised when her feet didn't hit the pavement immediately. She looked down at her size-12, double-narrow lace-up black boots. Was she losing gravity? Uh-oh. If she was losing gravity, she was losing humanity. If she was losing human-ity, vampness had the edge.

And why wouldn't it? I've been totally reckless, she thought. The more I revert to vampire ways, the harder they are to give up.

Lexie was so lost in her troubles, she hadn't noticed she'd passed her house.

Then she retraced her steps and saw why.

Where is our house? She bounced the message, hoping her brother or sister would catch it.

It's here, Hudson bounced back. *It's invisible is all. Feel your way.*

Easier bounced than done. Lexie tripped up the house's invisible steps and opened the invisible door, relieved to find that once inside, she could see the interior, sort of. All the furniture was cloaked in cobwebs and dust.

"Spit it out," Lexie demanded between sneezes. "What'd

you guys do to our home? Is this something you cooked up from the Old World *Handebooke offe Tryckes and Craftees?*"

"Maybe we slightly over-spelled." Maddy stood in the shadows, chewing her fingernails. Today her costume was Maid of Murder, a French maid's uniform, ketchup splattered, plus a rubber dagger. The morning's catchphrase had been, "Tend the bedding, then a beheading."

"*Slightly?* You made the house disappear. That's worse than turning it pixie pink." Lexie shook her head. "Mom and Dad will hit the roof."

"We'd wanted it de-varnished so it would look spookier. Instead, it vanished," complained Hudson, whose costume was a ghost made from eco-friendly hemp. "Haven't you ever messed up an Old World trick before?"

"Don't be a blunderhead," growled Lexie.

"Can you help us un-vanish the house?" asked Maddy. "Pul-eeeze?"

Usually, Lexie would have helped. That was the job of the oldest, to get the youngests out of a jam. Especially before the parents came home.

So she was surprised to hear herself say, "No. Also, I think you're both lumpish rubes to use that book so stupidly. Figure it out yourself."

Then she felt terrible. She'd never called her brother and sister names before. And now in less than one minute she'd used spiteful Old World insults like *blunderhead* and *lumpish rubes* to describe them.

Just as Pete had warned—she was using words like rocks.

Was it because of her extra vampness? If so, there was no time to dwell on it.

"Blix! Mitzi!" she called as she opened the door to her bedroom. "I might need some more dirt, this time on a girl named Riley Burnett."

"Shh!" Blix snapped. "You woke us up."

Lexie peered more closely at her bed. The pixies were taking a nap—but not as hedgehogs. They didn't look like pixies anymore, either. They'd grown taller, almost as tall as Lexie. They'd lost their wings. Except for his all-purple clothes and a purplish Mohawk, Blix resembled a regular kid. And Mitzi, whose peony pink jeans and glittery, baby pink T-shirt complemented her rosy pink cheeks, was utterly adorable.

"You're talking different," Lexie noticed out loud. "Not pixish."

"The New World is rubbing off on us," said Blix.

"And we've been siphoning all the spare human energy that you're giving off since you've 'fallen off the wagon'— again, as the humans say in slang," Mitzi added.

"Aha." Lexie hadn't realized that her discarded human energies were being recycled. The pixies were sneaky.

"Take us to your school tomorrow," said Mitzi, hopping over to Lexie's desk and handing her a folder. "Here's our signed paperwork so we can visit as students on a special permit from the country of Butterscratch."

"What? Butterscratch isn't even a real place." With a sinking heart, Lexie looked at the pix-forged documents, complete with seals and signatures. "Why do you want to go to Parrish? What do you want to learn at school?"

81

"Ugh, we don't want to learn anything," corrected Mitzi. "We're smart enough. We're just bored here is all."

"We want to play basketball and to help you gets— I mean *get*—more dirt." Blix's skin flushed grape with excitement.

Lexie looked from Blix to Mitzi. What a nightmare. How could things get worse than pixies at Parrish? "My life is officially out of control," Lexie murmured.

"We might need to borrow some of your clothes," mentioned Mitzi.

"And hair product," added Blix. "I like your watermelon-smelly glop."

"Oookay." I'll handle this whole mess, Lexie decided— the ex-pixie invasion, my lack of gravity, the invisible house, being a bad big sis, Pete Stubbe—*everything*, once the election's done. Then I'll reclaim my human touch, re-vegan my diet, and make up with everyone—maybe even including Mina.

But above and beyond anything, Lexie decided, she had to win the stupid election. Or at least get it over with because she couldn't bail out now. At this point, it had caused her too much capital *T* trouble.

"'Our visions begin with our desires,'" she said, quoting the poet Audre Lorde. She'd always liked that quote. The problem was, Lexie realized, she didn't have a clear vision *or* a clear desire. All she knew was she'd have to see this whole muddle through to its sweet—or bitter—end.

12

BUTTERSCRATCH AMBASSADORS

Good news. Our house re-visibilized," announced Maddy the next morning. "Thanks to our kook-tastic friend, Madame Peabody."

Lexie looked out the window. Sure enough, there it was.

"She came over early and put our house back on the map," said Hudson. "Then she showed us how to make spiderwebs, and how to grow mold for our haunted house, and how to build a zombie. Peabody's got a few inhuman tricks up her sleeve."

"Same as Lexie," murmured Maddy.

"Be quiet," Lexie growled as she reached for an orange and an apple. Her stomach rumbled. If only she could have some steak for breakfast. That would start the day out right. She knew it was a vampish thought, and she was surprised that she didn't much care. Maybe I've crossed the line, she thought. Maybe I'm not the same as "same old Lexie" anymore.

Maddy and Hudson had already finished breakfast and were outfitted in their Hallo-month costumes. This morning, Hudson was dressed as a shepherd, while Maddy was a ketchup-spattered pirate.

Lexie looked her up and down. "Let me guess your phrase of the day—'terror me timbers'?"

"I'm not that much of a blunderhead," said Maddy with a sniff. "And you better hurry up and finish your fruit or you'll make the pixies late for their first day at school."

Outside, the kids turned to walk their separate ways, Lexie, Mitzi—who was carrying a huge bouquet of roses—and Blix heading downtown to Parrish, while Maddy and Hudson veered uptown to P.S. 42. As they split off, Hudson said, "Hey, Lex, tomorrow I'm dressing up in a vampire costume. So I was thinking you can give me some tips. Since you're the vampest in the family."

"Whatever," Lexie snorted over her shoulder.

But no matter how she tried, throughout the day, she couldn't shake Maddy's and Hudson's comments. It seemed that she really had "fallen off the wagon," as Blix had told her. Even her little brother and sister sensed it.

At least, for today, the pixies were a busy distraction.

"Being a student might be harder than being a pixie," Lexie warned them as they checked in with the front office to present all their fake Butterscratch documents. "Especially algebra and writing-composition class."

"No math, no English," said Mitzi. "Just lunch and sports."

Lexie shook her head. "Good luck with that. Who are those roses for?"

"For the most popular Parrish person," answered Mitzi,

burying her nose in the bouquet. "We want to get in with the in crowd."

"That would be me," said Lexie. "I'm likely to win the class elec—"

"Welcome, Butterscratchian exchange students!" bellowed Ms. Oliphant, the school principal, bursting from her office to shake the pixies' hands. "What an honor. We hope you will enjoy your week at our school. Do you have any special requests or considerations?"

"We request extra sports and lunch," said Mitzi as Blix pulled out a pocket mirror and patted his stylish Mohawk.

Lexie left the pixies in Ms. Oliphant's hands.

Right from the start, it turned out that everyone loved the Butterscratch foreigners. Lexie was stunned by the pixies' ability to charm all the teachers and kids. They even sweet-talked Mina after Ms. Oliphant had deposited them in homeroom.

Only Mina, who had recognized the "visitors" from the fairy ring, was suspicious at first. "Hey. You're those crazy ballet kids. But you're so much taller," she noted. "How'd you pull that off?" Her eyes narrowed.

"It wasn't easy. And we hope our last encounter is all 'water under the bridge,'" said Mitzi. "We're sorry we got carried away with the Wiley Eye Rabbit. Our bones was—*were*—in great pain from our sudden, extreme growth spurt. Dancing was our only relief. Please accept our apology flowers." With a small bow, she offered Mina the bouquet.

Mina took it. "Thanks. At least now I know you're more with it than your host family," she said loudly. "Those Livingstones, especially Lexie, are ooky-spooky."

• • •

"What's your problem?" Lexie asked Blix and Mitzi later when she joined them for lunch. "I thought you hated Mina. After all, you helped wreck her campaign. You call her troll girl, remember?"

Mitzi shook her head. "We didn't like her when she was dressed up like a pixie. Now we see that she is an adorable human, with lots of natural bounce in her hair and irresistible dimples."

"I know *I* can't resist them. We want to be friends with her," added Blix.

"In fact, we were saving that chair for her." Mitzi pointed to the seat that Lexie was sitting in. "We are *sooo* all about Mina Pringle."

Lexie was upset but not surprised. After all, Orville had warned her that pixies were horribly disloyal.

Later, when Dylan came by to drop off some campaign toys, tiny little basketball nets with string-attached foam balls that read Pass the Vote to Dylan, the ex-pixies squealed and squawked.

"A present! A pixie present!" Mitzi clapped.

"Nobody ever gave us a present before!" Blix wiped a tear from his eye.

"Aw, that's too bad," said Dylan. "I thought you two were friends with Lexie."

"She never gave us a single present in her life," said Mitzi sadly.

"Lexie's a sweetheart," said Dylan. "I bet she'd give you a present on your birthday."

"No, no. Only walnuts or cupcakes. Lexie's a fartsmelt raisin chicken," said Blix. "So watch out."

Lexie couldn't think of a single quote in her defense as Dylan quickly left them to drop some campaign basketballs at the next table. Those pixies were the pits. More than ever, she missed her lunches with Pete, but these days he ate his sandwiches in the art room so that he could use the time to make signs about saving endangered species.

• • •

Throughout the week, as the pixies gained influence, they got increasingly on Lexie's nerves. They were so interested in showing kids how to style a Mohawk or how to talk backwards that they hardly had any time left over to help her with her campaign.

At least, like the election, the end was in sight.

"You know, M. and B., it's the final speeches tomorrow," Lexie reminded them that night as they ate cupcakes under her covers. "Did you ever get me any dirt on Riley Burnett?"

"Sorry, Lex," said Mitzi. "I didn't have time. Mina and

I ended up going shopping after school today. She's so cute. If Mina was a pixie, she'd have her pick of elf suitors lined ten toadstools deep to win her hand. I'm voting for her, no question."

"And I'm voting for Dylan Easterby," Blix confided, licking butterscotch frosting off his fingers. "If Dylan was a pixie, I'd let him ride my best winged unicorn to soccer practice."

"If Mina was pix, I'd brew her walnut stew every—"

"Enough, both of you!" Lexie looked up from her PHOLD. "You don't even go to Parrish. Kids can't be pixies, and Mr. Fellows won't let you vote, so end of discussion."

Blix nodded. "Not all true. Us—I mean *we*—changed Fellows's mind, didn't we, Mitzi?"

"Changed it? How?" asked Lexie.

In answer, the pixies traded a wink, finished their cupcakes, and fell asleep, leaving Lexie to fret through a long, sleepless night.

13

SPEECH, SPEECH!

Lexie was still fretting at the end of the next afternoon, when the student body filed into the auditorium for the final speeches. Mr. Fellows stood onstage at the podium. Mina, Neil, Lexie, Dylan, and Riley all sat behind him on folding chairs.

"Now, students," instructed Mr. Fellows. "Please hold your applause until each of our five candidates has spoken."

Everyone started to applaud anyway. Then Lexie noticed something fishy. On Mr. Fellows's feet were a pair of purple leather shoes, laced in pink silk ribbon.

"Quiet," said Mr. Fellows. "Each candidate has three minutes to speak. But first, our school anthem, led by Boris the Brown Badger."

He tapped his feet. Purple leather gleamed. Very suspicious.

Boris, who was really Mrs. Yoder in a brown badger costume, took the microphone. Lexie slipped out of her seat and offstage. She tugged on her teacher's arm. "Mr. Fellows," she whispered. "Where did you get those shoes?"

"Oh, these?" Mr. Fellows flushed. "Oddest thing. They were wrapped up in my mailbox the other day. From a secret admirer. Just my size, too."

"I think your secret admirers are Mitzi and Blix, so you'd let them vote."

Mr. Fellows's mustache trembled. "I'm the victim of a political conspiracy? That's unprecedented!"

"Take off your shoes and see how you feel."

Mr. Fellows slipped off his shoes and then checked out Blix and Mitzi, who were easy to spy in the audience since they glowed with a pastel luminescence that no other Parrish students could replicate with makeup or clothing. "You're right, Lexie, they shouldn't vote. They're only visitors."

He slid the shoes back on. "Okay, now I think they should vote."

"See? It's a trick. An old pix . . . I mean, Butterscratch trick."

"But they're such lovely shoes," said Mr. Fellows. He bent and retied the laces. "Go back to your seat, Lexington. And may the best candidate win."

"So does that mean they get to vote?"

"Of course. I have no intention of walking around barefoot all day."

Lexie returned to her chair with lead in her feet and a wrench in her stomach.

Mina spoke first. Ducks, fountains, and Fizzle Nuts. "And remember, friends—I'm the candidate who's creating the OTLE plan. It stands for *option to leave early,* and it means kids get to tell volunteers to go home. First order of business—we're gonna OTLE the Yoder. Yep, I said it— and you know I'll do it, too. Thanks, darlings!"

On her way back to her seat, Mina stepped hard on Lexie's foot. When Lexie squeaked, the auditorium roared with laughter.

Dylan's speech was fun. He yelled and whooped and pumped his fist in the air. On his way back to his chair, he also stepped on Lexie's foot—but not to hurt. Just to make the kids laugh again. Which they did.

Lexie hobbled to the podium. Everyone just wants to be entertained, she thought grimly. Nobody cares about my policies. Not even me. Her one-minute-long speech reminded everyone not to trust Mina, though she couldn't totally remember the reason why. "In conclusion, many are called, but few are chosen. In this case, choose me. Thanks."

"Somebody is boring me, and I think it's me," she quoted to herself sadly as she slunk back to her seat.

Neil was next. He outlined his plan for how to have an in-service day at Parrish on alternate weekends. He got some boos. He talked about fire drills. Nobody listened.

By the time Riley Burnett took the stage, kids had become restless and chatty. Mr. Fellows had to ask for quiet three times.

Riley's voice was very soft, to match her mousy looks.

"Speak up!" shouted Blake Chapman, a senior.

Riley coughed. Then started again. "*Dag, labass, selam, welina*, and hey to everyone," she said, loud and clear. "You all know me as Riley, the new girl with the funny accent. What you might not know is my parents work for the United Nations. Since kindergarten, I've lived in seven different countries." She stopped and smiled. She had a warm smile. "I've seen how lots of schools work, and I wanted to share some thoughts based on my different experiences. So here's one: let's sign up for online classrooms, like at my old school in Hong Kong, where we interact with our global community. We can learn from them, and they can learn from us. I know this is a speech but—any thoughts?"

"I like that idea," spoke up Miss Evans, the new chemistry teacher, who was sitting in the front row. "I've been campaigning for that since September."

"Cool. Let's talk after. Idea two." Riley paused. "Rainwater. Did you know our school's got a flat roof? We can harvest gallons of fresh water to filter and reuse. And it worked at my school in Frankfurt."

The room was abuzz about the flat roof, fresh rain, and Frankfurt. Riley's voice gained volume.

"And here's another idea. Let's make a compost heap from lunch scraps, like in my school in Akureyri, to create an organic garden. We'll build it off the courtyard and share the fresh veggies all year."

"Ew." Mina sniggered. "Compost." But Lexie could see in the audience that kids enjoyed the idea of a garden in the courtyard. Her own mouth was watering. Fresh-picked tomatoes every day. Yum.

"Oh, and here's something else," Riley continued. "At my old school in Halifax, we had a student radio program where kids could call in and just talk about—well, anything, really. I hope you'll take a chance on me: 'Riley with a smiley.' Thank you, *arigato, merci, asai, spasibo, gracias.*"

Riley hopped from the podium and returned to her seat.

Then Mr. Fellows came center stage. "That's it. Thanks, everyone, for coming to the debates," he said. "And thanks to our ambassadors from Butterscratch for their visit. One day, perhaps one of us will have the honor of visiting you and voting in *your* student election." He clicked his purple heels.

Lexie shuffled dispiritedly out of the auditorium. She'd just witnessed a true politician up at that podium, and her name was Riley Burnett.

The sound was faint at first. Then her ear homed in on it. It was the hum of an insect, bumping around the back hall to the music rooms. A mosquito? Mmm. Right now, a mosquito sounded even better than a bee pollen smoothie.

She darted down the hall. Listening. Searching. Where was it? She careened into rooms. The sound was fainter. It must have escaped through a window. Lexie pushed through the fire escape door into a back alley lined with trash cans.

Nope. There was no mosquito out here.

She jumped as the claw fell heavy on her shoulder.

"Lost your way?" intoned the voice.

"Orville!" He'd been perched in wait on the fire escape. "You scared me."

"Lexington," said Orville, "you have gravely disappointed me."

93

"You? Me?" Lexie squeaked. "How? Why?" Was Orville joking? Was this a Halloween prank? But no, the old creature looked dead serious.

"I think you know why. These past weeks, you've rejected everything that you, as an on-your-way-to-human being, should have valued most." Orville's hooded eyes blinked in reproach. "Is your ancient nature an unbreakable force?"

"I don't know," said Lexie. "Is it?"

"That's for you to decide. All we know is that you've resorted to vampire traits of heartlessness and vengefulness. In fact, you are on the brink of becoming . . ." He paused. "Nocturnal."

"No." Lexie's voice was hardly more than breath. Not nocturnal. Anything but that. Had she really regressed so much? It wasn't a complete surprise. "B-but then I won't be able to go to sc-school at all," she stuttered. "I'll be awake all night and asleep all day. Everything will be so upside down." And so lonely. So unbearable.

"If you're not tired tonight, then it's already happened," Orville admitted. "But either way, you should start work now. To reclaim."

"Reclaim what?" Lexie faltered.

Orville ruffled his feathers. "Reclaim humanity, of course. In fact, I can think of a few individuals that you've hurt on your path to victory."

"Oh, right," mustered Lexie. But she wasn't sure who Orville was talking about.

Suddenly, the fire escape door banged open, and an

irate Dylan stood before her. "Aha. I *thought* that was you I saw through the window. Lexie, you've gone too far." He shook his finger. His green eyes blazed.

Lexie quaked. "Whatever it is, I didn't do it."

"Don't lie. I know you were behind this!" He held up a poster board.

The giant, blow-up picture was of Dylan in his underwear, practicing a karate kick. His face was scrunched, his kick was crooked, and his underwear had a design of lassos and cowboy hats on it.

It might have been possible for him to look like a bigger idiot, but Lexie didn't see how. "I—I didn't take that picture," she stammered.

There was a brush of wings against her back as Orville swooped off.

"Course you did. It's the same photo stunt you pulled with Mina. Do you think I'm just some dumb jock who doesn't know how sneaky you are?" Dylan scoffed. "I used to think you were cool, Lexie. But you've redefined that word for me. You're a creepy, obnoxious, obsessed loser. That's how cool you are."

14

THE DARK SIDE

Orville had warned Lexie that if she didn't feel tired to-night, she could say good-bye to her human sleep. She'd be nocturnal until she'd saved up enough exceptional human behavior. Which could be months.

And it was all because of this miserable election.

"Enjoy your *spoooky* visit." Lexie's father wiggled his eyebrows. Tonight Lexie had promised to bring Maddy and Hudson over to Madame Peabody's house to get some haunted-house tips from her. It was the last thing Lexie wanted to do, but it would take her mind off the Dylan fiasco. Besides, she hadn't been much of a big sister these days.

"If you need help, just call us," said the pixies, who were sitting at the kitchen table, making buttons for Dylan's and Mina's campaign.

"No, thanks," said Lexie. "Your last 'help' was to plaster those terrible posters of Dylan all over the school. He was so angry with me, I don't think we'll ever be friends."

"That was all me," admitted Mitzi proudly. "But it was to save Mina's campaign. I didn't think about yours. Mina and Dylan are competing for the popular vote."

"Well, Dylan despises me. There's not even a quote

96

for how sad I am," said Lexie as her eyes prickled with tears.

The pixies giggled softly. But they didn't mock Lexie when they saw they'd upset her. And they didn't touch the cupcakes that Lexie's father whipped up after Lexie refused to make them any. "We'll grant you any secret wish," called Mitzi as they trooped out the door. "No joke."

"Whatever." It was just more pixie propaganda, thought Lexie. With Hudson on one side and Maddy on the other, she set off down the block for Madame's house.

"Like my costume? I'm a vintage vampire," said Hudson. "This is Dad's old nightwalker outfit from back in the day." He squeezed Lexie's hand. "Sorry I called you the most vampish, Lex. Thanks for coming out with us tonight."

"No prob, Hud. I guess I *have* been creepier than usual," Lexie admitted. "I need to get back on the straight and narrow."

"Did you notice that I'm a magician?" asked Maddy, swirling her cape. "I put disgusting in the pockets, too. Just in case."

At the Peabody house, the lights were low. Lexie pressed the buzzer, setting off a chime to the tune of "Silver Bells." The front door opened immediately.

"Hello! You must be Lexie. Lovely to meet you." Madame Astrid Peabody presented a round silver tray. "May I offer you a pig in a blanket?"

"What a horrifying food," whispered Hudson as they all

declined. "It's pastry and pork." He looked frightened. "Good start to the night of fright for vegetarians, Madame P."

"Oopsie! My mistake." Madame withdrew her tray. "No matter, there are cucumber finger sandwiches in the drawing room." She beckoned. "Come in and meet my sister, Petunia, who is visiting from, ah, elsewhere."

"Sandwiches made from fingers," murmured Maddy. "Gross. I like it."

They filed after Madame into the drawing room, where a few easels and canvases had been set up. A woman who looked like Madame, except younger, was lounging on a love seat. Her lap was full of crickets, and her eyes were black as bullets.

"This is my sister, Petunia," said Madame.

"Greetings," said Petunia.

"Please sit," said Madame, "but keep your kiesters off my ladybugs, crickets, and spiders. They run loose through the house. I'm an entomologist, if you haven't guessed already."

"Oh, that's interesting, because people in the neighborhood think you're a witch," Maddy mentioned before Lexie could elbow her.

Petunia Peabody cackled. "Our house might be fearsome, but my sister wouldn't hurt a flea," she said. "Or a bug."

Hudson pointed to the walls, which were hung with many paintings. Lexie looked. One painting was of dogs playing poker. Another was of fairies sitting on toadstools.

The largest painting was of a cemetery, where a black-velvet-dressed figure was climbing out of an open grave.

"I painted the graveyard scene," said Petunia with pride. "I used glow-in-the-dark paints."

"My sister is so imaginative," said Madame. "And her horrible painting got me thinking—why don't we paint some scary pictures for your haunted house? A few paintings like Petunia's will spook everyone."

The Livingstones didn't need to be asked twice. They all whipped on smocks and got to work. Hudson painted winged demons. Maddy painted a vicious Old World Knaveheart, most terrifying of all pureblood vampires, eating a rat. Lexie painted the tragic death of Anne Boleyn. Eventually Madame fell asleep in her armchair. Maddy and Hudson finished their scary paintings and started up a round of yawning contests. Only Lexie and Petunia remained wide awake.

Lexie shivered as the thought crossed her mind. Was Petunia also a Nocturnal?

"Since you're all half asleep, why don't you all stay the night?" suggested Petunia as she put away her paintbrushes. "My sister seems to be a goner."

"Good idea." Lexie faked a stretch. "I'll text my parents." In truth, all her vamp senses were on alert. There was something odd—maybe even dangerous—about Petunia. Was it her extra-vamp instincts that made her want to fight instead of flee?

They followed Petunia up the stairs and down the corridor. Her waist-length hair swished against her black gown, creating a hypnotic rustling sound.

Swish, swish, swish.

"Call if you need anything, I'm just at the other end of the hall," Petunia told them after she showed them to their rooms. Another hair swish and she closed the door.

"I'm sooo tired," said Maddy.

"Me too," admitted Hudson. He flipped himself upside down on the closet rail and promptly fell asleep.

Maddy crawled into one of the twin beds and pulled up the covers. Lexie noticed that she hadn't even taken off her shoes. "I used to think Madame Peabody was a vampire, but she's too wrinkly," said Maddy. "Also, she's got tons of silver lying around. She's even wearing silver rings. I think," with a final yawn, "that Madame's just a sweet, semi-retired witch. And you can never have too many of those in the neighborhood." With that, she fell sound asleep.

From Hudson's closet came the sound of snoring.

But Lexie wasn't sleepy. Not at all. Yes, Madame Peabody was weird. But Petunia Peabody was worse than weird. And if Lexie had to put money on who the vampire in the Peabody clan was . . .

She took her compact from her bag and slipped it in her pocket as she climbed into the other bed. She made herself shut her eyes. Keeping her neck exposed and every muscle flexed, she waited.

• • •

Crrrrrrrrirdkkkkk.

The guest-room door creaked open.

Lexie's ears pricked as someone approached. She hoped her moonlit neck would draw the creature closer, and she was right. Now she could feel the brush of black silk hair against her cheek and the pearly tip of a fang—

"Gotcha!" Lexie jumped up and brandished the compact, but the silver-backed case burned hot in her palm. Because I'm too vampish to touch a mirror! she realized. Wincing, she nevertheless managed to beam the mirror straight at Petunia Peabody's terrified face.

"Eeeeeee!" Petunia's pale fingers flew to her skin, which had already started to splinter like a teacup.

"Ha! I knew it!" Lexie waggled a finger. "Begone, deadly fullblood!"

"Drop that right now!" Petunia reached out, pawing for the compact. Petunia was no shrinking flower, Lexie realized with dismay as the compact fell from her hand and crashed onto the floor.

Maddy and Hudson slept on.

"You spelled them," accused Lexie, "with your swishy hair."

"Exactly. It's an Old World trick but a good one," croaked Petunia, crushing the compact beneath her high-heeled shoe. "But why didn't my enchantment work on you?"

"I'm nocturnal," said Lexie. "Too vampish for your tricks. Why didn't you crumble to dust from the mirror?"

"Because," said Petunia, with an extra twist of her stiletto, "I'm a Back-to-the-Old-World fullblood."

"What's that?" Lexie had never heard of such a thing.

As Petunia advanced inch by inch on Lexie, she explained. "About fifty years ago, Astrid and I emigrated as fullblood vampires from the Old World to try our fortunes here. We swore off bloodsucking for good. Astrid became a renowned scientist, and twenty years later, she gained mortality. But I couldn't let go of my deviant ways. The coffin bed, the warm bloody drinks, ahhh. I deeply missed the drama, the intrigue, and especially the terror on the faces of my helpless victims.

"After a few run-ins with the Argos, I returned to the Old World and swore to eternal vampirism. That's when I redoubled my power." Petunia arched her brow and stepped closer. "Is that what you are? Half vamp but unable to reform?"

"No." Lexie stepped back. "I'm a fruit-bat hybrid who wants to turn mortal. But I've lost my way a little."

Petunia smirked. "That's what I used to say. Darling, you've strayed far from your school yard, haven't you? So let me take you all the way to the dark side. Some hybrids are simply less human than others. Here's my plan. Allow me to bite you. I'll drink most of your blood, then give you some of mine."

"That works?" asked Lexie.

"As long as you don't resist. If you agree to accept the bite, it's nontoxic. It will infuse you with powers, such as bat-morphing. When we return to the Old World, you'd finally be received as a real, diabolical vampire—not just a wimpy fruit hybrid. And you can visit your family once a year, though you'll have to watch them get old while you stay eternally gorgeous." Petunia's fingertips touched her crackly face. "Hurry up and decide. I despise looking chipped, and I need a blood fix to repair my face."

"Let me open the window," said Lexie. "This is a lot of information. I better get some fresh air so that I can think."

Petunia herself threw open the window on the strength of a single pinkie finger. "See how strong I am? You could be, too."

"Pleh." Lexie nodded. "Pleh, pleh."

Petunia squinched her nose. "Is that slang? New World talk is so trendy."

"Pleh em, Xilb dna Iztim," said Lexie.

Petunia frowned. "What are you—" But she had no time to finish her sentence because she was too busy screaming bloody murder. "AAAEEEEE!"

Lexie could only stumble back in horror as Petunia's hair yanked bolt up from her scalp, tugging her through the air and all the way to the ceiling light, where it wrapped itself into a knot that left the rest of her dangling.

"GRUESOME PIXIES!" Petunia screeched. "Where did you come from?!" Her fingers pulled desperately to free herself as the pixies began to dance below her. "Release me at once!" Her spindly legs churned.

"What's all this racket?" The bedroom door opened and Madame Peabody stood in the door frame, covered in bugs and blinking. "Petunia! Why are you hanging from the light?"

"Astrid, you nincompoop, I didn't do it to myself! The pixies tied me!"

"Pixies? But who invited pixies here?"

"The Livingstone brats! Don't you realize that they're hybrids? Untie me and bring me a kid to bite! I need blood!"

Madame Peabody shook her head. "Sister, dear, you know I don't like getting mixed up in your biting business."

Petunia hissed as she turned on Lexie. "I'm not going to hang here forever, and when I get down, I'll have my revenge on one of your sleeping siblings."

"No!" said Lexie. "Don't you dare hurt them! Bite me instead, and take me back to the Old World. I—I'm ready for the dark side."

"*Now* you're talking sense." Petunia sneered.

Lexie closed her eyes and quickly made her silent wish to the pixies. *Blix and Mitzi, just one trick. Give me wings to make me quick. A fullblood's sure to win this fight unless I land a perfect bite.*

Instantly, she could feel the itch between her shoulder blades as, hummingbird-style, fluted pixie wings sprouted from them. Lexie darted to the ceiling and, quick as an antique record needle, dropped her fangs into Petunia's cracked, unwilling neck.

"STAArgh!" The vampire writhed as her hair unslithered from its knot and she dropped to the floor like a sack of salt. Mitzi and Blix squealed in fear as they rolled to safety under the heater.

Lexie's fangs zinged as she retreated, hovering in the air.

Was one hybrid bite enough to take out a fullblood? Probably not, and it wasn't more than a moment before Petunia had staggered back up on her stilettos and came after Lexie, growling. "You will pay!"

Terrified, Lexie swooped down, grabbing a shard of compact mirror to hold up like a shield to protect herself. Petunia lunged, her fingers ripping the thin tissue of Lexie's wing as she fluttered to the safety of the windowsill, nearly bumping against the creature that had been perched in darkness there.

Her heart caught in her throat. "Oh! Who are . . . ?"

But the creature had already leaped straight for Petunia, pinning her to the floor. Lexie's heart pounded as she watched the vampire struggle with the beast. The jabbering pixies, sensing Petunia's imminent defeat, found their courage and leaped back out to finish her off in trademark pixie fashion, yanking at her gray hair so that it fell out in straggly clumps.

"Eeeeeeee, my hair! My lustrous hair!" Clutching her scalp, Petunia was fast becoming more crumbles than creature. "You're destroying my crowning beauty!"

"Good-bye, fullblood," squealed the pixies, who then chanted, "You thought you'd easily trounce a pixie, but you didn't know 'bout Blix 'n' Mitzi."

A pop, a poof, and then Petunia was no more than a heap of pink dust.

Moonlight spilled from behind a cloud and flooded the bedroom.

"Ooh." And now Lexie recognized the helpful beast—

105

even in his wolfish state. "Pete!" she whispered. "How did you find me?"

"You called for help," he said. "I speak backwardsian, too. Sorry I was too late to the battle, but I was at a Save the Polar Bears vigil."

"No biggie," said Lexie. "We got the job done, and Maddy and Hudson didn't even wake up for it."

"You're lucky to have such talented friends," said Madame Peabody as the pixies took a bow. "My sister had it coming. She really was so diabolical. A terrible sister to the end. She used to slather my darling crickets on her steak."

Lexie shuddered. Not one particle of her being was in the mood for a steak. That bite of Petunia would put her off meat for a long, long time, and she knew her other vampish urges were, thankfully, dormant. For now.

"Wonderful pixies," she praised, "thank you for granting my wish for wings. I didn't think I could count on you in a pinch."

"Us has heart," said Blix with a shrug. He swirled a finger, and Lexie's wings disappeared.

"Now you owe cupcakes," added Mitzi. "Your dad's ones stink." And they swept out of the window, heading back to the Livingstones' townhouse.

"Good night, dear," said Madame Peabody. "I hope you want to stay human. My sister's life was more glamorous, but mine has been rich with mortal interests. Now come along, my buggy loves." In a twitch of shiny wings and waving antennae, she shuffled back to bed.

Lexie gave her dear wolf friend a hug. Because the best reason to want mortality was right in front of her. That and the heap of dust that had been Petunia. A gruesome, violent death was just one of the downsides of being full-blood vamp. And yet it was a vampire's violent life, Lexie realized, that she especially disdained.

"My trip to the dark side is officially over," she said.

Leaving Maddy and Hudson to sleep off their spell, Pete and Lexie climbed up to Madame Peabody's roof for a quiet view of the city.

When Lexie finally spoke, she made sure her words were the opposite of rocks. "Pete, I'm sorry I haven't been a good friend to you these past weeks."

Pete shifted to rest his chin on her knee. "I'm sorry right back, Lex. I got too caught up with Crunchee. But you can't forfeit your old peeps just because you've found someone new. And I guess I was so into saving other species, I didn't see how our friendship was going extinct."

"Never." Lexie yawned. Was she tired? She was tired! She yawned again for the joy of it. "I might take a nap out here, but let's make sure we wake up by sunrise. After all, I've got cupcakes to bake."

15

MUCHO HALLOWEENO

At sunrise, Pete dropped off the Livingstones at their house, now freshly painted a color between pink and purple.

"Mitzi and Blix's parting gift," said their mother. "They asked you to ship them their final cupcakes. They said it was time to start their country life."

"I like the house this color," Lexie decided.

"Good, since I think it's permanent," said Lexie's father.

Lexie smiled. The mauve house would be a pleasant reminder of Mitzi and Blix, who'd proven their loyalty in the end.

"Hey there, Orville," said Lexie as she arrived in her bedroom to find the creature waiting worriedly at her window. "Guess what? I had a good sleep last night. It's just that I slept on a roof, not in a bed."

"Glad to hear it." The old creature looked genuinely relieved as he offered her a green Granny Smith apple. "Here. It's important to start today off right."

"Why's that?" Lexie asked with a crunch.

"It's Halloween *and* your class election," reminded Orville.

The election! She'd forgotten! She didn't even have a costume—except for Maddy's vampire cape. Well, it would have to do.

Downstairs, Lexie found her brother and sister already outfitted in their grand-finale Halloween costumes.

"The Maddy Hatter." Lexie nodded. "I like it, Mads. It's more sly than scary. What's your catchphrase?"

Her sister smiled. "My catchphrase is 'one dollar, please.' Since that's what Hudson and I are charging for a tour of our spectacular haunted house."

"Good times at Madame Peabody's, huh?" added Hudson. "We made some awesomely gruesome paintings, and her closet makes a perfect sleep den."

Lexie stared at her little brother. "Hud, what's your costume?"

Hudson twirled his velvet dress that was covered in paper ladybugs. "I'm Petunia Peabody." He tossed his silky black wig.

"She doesn't really look like that anymore," said Lexie, but Hudson and Maddy had no memory of what happened at the Peabody house after they'd fallen asleep. Just as well, thought Lexie. Her fangs still ached. Being extra vamp had saved them from Petunia, but she'd had enough of the dark side to last a lifetime.

Now it was time to repair some more damage. And she wouldn't be waiting until the elections were over.

"I made a mistake," she said to herself. "But what can I say? I'm only human." Well, almost only.

At school, tensions were running high. Lexie was dismayed that Dylan kept his distance from her. His glare spoke volumes.

Mina, on the other hand, bounced right up. "Hello, Yucktopus. Brave costume choice. As if you don't look enough like a vampire already, you've got to add a cape." Mina herself was dressed in her peachy ballerina tutu.

"I'm only a pretend vampire," said Lexie. "I've got nothing to hide."

"Sell it all you want," Mina sniped, "but you're not a regular person, Lexie. You've got plenty to hide, and when I find out, I'm telling."

"Your bark is worse than your bite," said Lexie, "but I'm not sure you can say the same thing about me. Good luck with the election." And for a moment, less than one-tenth of a second, she made her eyeballs go ice clear. Just to turn one lemony yellow hair on Mina's head prematurely gray.

Lexie's eyes changed back to brown so quick, Mina didn't know what had happened. But she backed away from Lexie, shaking her head.

Once a vamp, always a vamp. Guess I'm still a work in progress until I'm one hundred percent human, Lexie decided. And that would have to do.

Mr. Fellows tallied votes at lunch, and he made the announcement after recess. Fifty percent of the votes had gone to Riley Burnett, while the other fifty percent had been divided among Dylan, Mina, Lexie, and Neil.

And so it ends, thought Lexie with relief.

"My first order of business," declared a flushed and

victorious Riley, "is to appoint my dream cabinet. If you're interested, here's my proposal."

Lexie was in-class poet resident and official speech-writer.

Dylan was sports and leisure captain.

Mina was social chair.

Neil Needleburger was vice president.

"I'm honored," said Neil after much clearing of his throat.

"A unified cabinet of former political rivals is unprecedented," Mr. Fellows commented. "Which means Riley is setting a precedent. Nice job, Riley."

"There's a Halloween party at my house after school," said Lexie to Mina. "Will you officially announce it? Since you're social chair."

"Uh, okay," Mina answered, giving Lexie a skeptical eye.

"I hope you'll come," Lexie added. "I've got something to show you."

Mina shrugged as if she didn't care, but Lexie could see she was curious. So was Dylan when she told him. "I might have other plans," he said stiffly.

"I understand," Lexie answered, "but I'd love you to be there. I think you'll get a kick out of it—no pun intended."

Back at the house, the Livingstones went to work. First, they set up their Rogues Gallery of their spooky paintings—with a few surprises thrown in. The main one was a blown-up photograph of Lexie, taken three months ago, when she had dressed up as a stalk of broccoli to promote the Broccoli Blast smoothie at the Candlewick Café. It had been the first photograph that she'd ever shown up in, and she had always been extremely proud of it.

"It's scary how embarrassed I feel for you," said Hudson.

"You sure about this, Lex?" asked Maddy.

"Yep. I've got the dirt on myself, and I'm not afraid to rub it in."

Soon Madame Peabody arrived with Petunia's paintings. "It's a final tribute, I suppose. Her first and last gallery showing," she said.

"She'd be proud of how many kids it's going to scare," said Maddy. "Want to sample some horrifying food, Madame? A finger sandwich, perhaps?"

"Oh! They're in the shape of real fingers," said Madame. "I think I'll pass."

"Your house is beautiful!" cried Riley Burnett, who was next to come over along with her new governing cabinet. "Just like on New Providence Island. All the houses there are painted in a sunset palette."

Now that's a good politician, thought Lexie. Riley knew how to say exactly the right thing at exactly the right moment.

"Step right up," invited Hudson, "and see the famous Livingstone Haunted House. It's packed with eco-friendly thrills and chills."

"One dollar, please," said Maddy, cutting in front of Hudson, and there she stayed as more kids turned onto the Livingstones' street corner.

"You're charging us, too?" asked a spotted owl, who stood hand in hand with a manatee. "But we're endangered."

"Sorry," said Maddy. "No discounts for rare species."

Lexie peered closer. "Woo-hoot, stranger. You almost had me."

Pete the owl grinned, enjoying his disguise as a whole other nocturnal creature.

"Which means," said Lexie, turning to the manatee, "you must be Crunchee."

"That's my environmental name." The manatee nodded and lifted her mask. "Though you might also know me as—"

"Get out! Kaylee Milquetoast!" Lexie blinked in amazement as she peered into the famous face of the actress-singer. Then she put a finger to her lips. "Don't let *anyone* know you're here," she whispered. "Some people want you to be our new school mascot."

Frightened, Crunchee-Kaylee re-hid behind her manatee mask.

"Come on in, both of you. You won't be disappointed." And even if Lexie's heart tugged since she knew that Pete wasn't going to be all hers, all the time, she made sure her friend didn't see it.

"We've got a hit on our hands with this house," said Hudson. "A perfect end to Hallo-month."

Lexie had to agree. The horrible paintings, cobwebs, squeaky doors, spare coffins, turnaround bookcases, and rusty armor on the walls had kids roaming everywhere, gasping and ahhhing. Madame had even rigged the piano to play by itself.

Maddy's moldy room was of particular interest. "Who could live in such a mildewed mess?" Kids shook their heads in disgust, then screamed as Madame's remote-controlled pop-out zombie came careening out of her closet.

"The peach-blossom parrot can live anywhere," spoke a voice behind Lexie as kids stampeded out in search of the next thrill. "And you always know he's comfortable if he sleeps with one foot up."

Lexie turned. "You came!"

Mina gave a small smile. "Loo texted and sent me your broccoli picture. I had to see it myself."

"Loo sent it to me, too," said Dylan. "I think she sent it to the whole school."

"Dylan." Lexie couldn't hide her delight. "Glad you changed your mind."

"Way to embarrass yourself," he said, showing the snap of Lexie the broccoli on his phone. "You look like a world-class goober in that outfit."

"Seriously, Lexie, you're such a freak. I'm amazed that you hang out with hipster kids like Mitzi and Blix," added Mina. "Are they here? I wanted to invite them to my Fourth of July party. Better book them early before they make other plans."

"They went back to Butterscratch," said Lexie. Then she waited, fingers crossed.

But Mina just tossed her curls and did a quick pirouette. "Mmm, I smell something good."

"Mexican appetizers," said Lexie quietly. "They're very savory, if you'd like to try some."

As they trooped downstairs, Dylan took her hand. "Sweet party, Lex."

"Thanks."

Mina was the only girl whose invitation snub could crush her. And Dylan was the only guy whose hand squeeze could give her that throw-uppy-in-a-good-way feeling. Mortal life was so complicated. Still, she wouldn't trade it for all the eternity in the world.

The Livingstones didn't find out about the fate of the pixies until a month or so later, when Lexie picked up the mail.

A flyer advertising for the "Wildflower Inn" showed a photograph of an upstate country inn with a shimmering pink-and-purple sunset behind it. On the back of the card was scrawled: *Come visit. Sends us cupcakes. M. & B.*

"What a darling inn," said her mother. "Maybe your father and I will grab a getaway weekend."

Lexie scrutinized the card. "This image could have been pixi-morphed."

"What's a piximorph?" asked her mother.

"A prank." Lexie smiled. "Nothing that you'd ever want to do to anybody." Then she grabbed a shiny apple from the fruit bowl, tucked her PHOLD under her arm, and went off to be inspired.

Poems

Though I am but
a fruit-bat lass,
Whose skin crisps
'neath a noonday sky,
I plant my skinny feet
on grass—
so vamp-ambitions
touch the sky!

Hopes

I hope Dylan
realizes that
we are meant
to be.

Opinions

Butterscotch
cupcakes taste
better with
sprinkles!

Lyrics

"Everything falls apart
and the grass will grow
as surely as they will
break your heart."

-Joy Division

Dreams

I dreamed I danced
a perfect tango.

The Stolen Child

by W. B. Yeats

Where dips the rocky highland
Of Sleuth Wood in the lake,
There lies a leafy island
Where flapping herons wake
The drowsy water-rats;
There we've hid our faery vats,
Full of berries
And of reddest stolen cherries.
Come away, O human child!
To the waters and the wild
With a faery, hand in hand,
For the world's more full of weeping
than you can understand.

© lexiedoodles

How To Spot A Pixie In Your School

purple or pink tint in eyes

loves slang phrases

he will <u>not</u> share his cupcakes

pocket full of walnuts

shoes curl up

Strange Rumors Abounded...

- Letitia had as many friends as she did enemies
- She was in perfect health . . . until her morning coffee
- Her death was ruled a cyanide poisoning. Accident? Suicide? Murder?

Who Killed Letitia E. Landon?

HOW I GET ALL THE ATTENTION IN THE ROOM

I think quick by drinking power smoothies

I only give a hint of ear

I stay poetic

I reflect honestly

I practice karate

I kick it with stylin' stompy boots

My Secrets Revealed

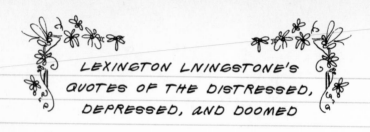

LEXINGTON LIVINGSTONE'S
QUOTES OF THE DISTRESSED,
DEPRESSED, AND DOOMED

"So many gods, so many creeds / So many paths that wind and wind, / While just the art of being kind / Is all the sad world needs."   —Ella Wheeler Wilcox (1850–1919)

"I know not who these mute folk are / Who share the unlit place with me— / Those stones out under the low-limbed tree / Doubtless bear names that the mosses mar."
                                        —Robert Frost (1874–1963)

"Come away, O human child! / To the waters and the wild / With a faery, hand in hand, / For the world's more full of weeping than you can understand."
                                        —William Butler Yeats (1865–1939)

"He that readeth good writers and pickes out their flowres for his own nose is lyke a foole."
                                        —Stephen Gosson (1554–1624)

"A man without a vote is a man without protection."
                                        —Lyndon B. Johnson (1908–1973)

"Bad officials get elected by good citizens who do not vote."   —George Jean Nathan (1882–1958)

"Our visions begin with our desires."

— Audre Geraldine Lorde (1934–1992)

"Ay, now by all the bitter tears / That I have shed for thee, / The racking doubts, the burning fears, / Avenged they well may be." — Letitia Elizabeth Landon (1802–1838)

"Some leaders are born women." — Unknown

"Don't be too timid and squeamish about your actions. All life is an experiment. The more experiments you make, the better." — Ralph Waldo Emerson (1805–1882)

"Somebody's boring me. I think it's me." — Dylan Thomas (1914–1953)

ORIGINAL POEMS
BY LEXIE LIVINGSTONE

MORTAL BELOVED:
AN ELEGY TO NATHANIEL RHINEBECK,
AKA FUN K. BLOOD (1987-2009)

I'd buy a day if you were in it.
I'd pay in gold to re-begin it.
Fun K., you were hotter than a toaster.
Your face was on my coolest poster.
I'd like to spin Time all around,
Bring back Fun K. safe and sound.
But fugu poison sealed your fate.
They say you hardly touched your plate.
Like mushroom cap and rhubarb leaf,
One taste foretells untimely grief.
I wish I'd warned you on this dish—
You cannot mess with poison fish.
— L.L.

ODE TO ODIOUS PIXIES

My day was gold, my outlook sunny,
Mina's friendship almost sealed.
They pinked our house and thought it funny—
What pesky power pixies wield.
My campaign plan was lame and hazy,
My heart just wasn't in this race.
But pixies made it mean and crazy—
Can I step down with any grace?
Greedy pixies love their sweets
and will not share one nibble.
Next time I mix their cupcake treats—
I'll add some doggie kibble.
— L.L.

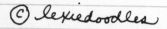